BLOOD IS SILENT

BLOOD IS SILENT

RED RIDING HOOD IS A CIRCUS AERIALIST...
THE WOLF HAS PLANS FOR HER

K.M. ROBINSON

To those that dare to soar.

CHAPTER ONE

"You need to worry more about the world," he warns as his eyes flick over to me. "You're not invincible, Sienna."

"Neither are you, Ephraim."

He eyes me with a grin. "Actually, that's exactly what I am, madam." Ephraim motions down to his abs as he tightens them.

"Just because they advertise you as the Invincible Man, doesn't mean you are, Eph. I've seen you in training, don't forget."

Spinning, I twirl my silks around me like a cape, clutching it under my chin. I consider sticking my tongue out at him but decide to pretend to be mature instead.

"I don't think that's how that's supposed to be used." He smirks.

"How would *you* know? You're on the ground all the time."

I wrap my foot around the fabric and begin to climb using my other foot to hold the fabric in place, pushing myself higher as Ephraim watches me. My hands and feet take turns pushing and pulling my body into position.

"You've had me in the air enough times that I can *pretend* to do your job, Sienna."

"Yes, and flawless as you may be, I still look prettier up here," I counter playfully. I separate the silks and lift myself up into a double foot lock. Josephine starts the organ music across the tent as we all warm up for the evening's show. It's muggy in the tent and the crickets have started chirping early this evening.

"Indeed." Ephraim turns and makes his way over to a bench where he starts curling his arms as he lifts his weights, showing off as several of the girls walk by. They ignore me in favor of ogling Ephraim.

Can't he just practice throwing knives instead? He has more than one job here.

"Where is she?" An icy voice cuts through the organ's deep tones.

Turning, I find Samuel standing in front of me. I lift both hands above my head, leaning forward as I cross the silks behind my back. Moving my hands to grasp the fabric, I lean back to invert, legs out to the side as I dangle upside down from the silks.

"Who?" I reply, facing away from him.

"Ida, of course," he snaps. "She's been gone for three days. Where is she?"

"You know as well as I do that she's out in the woods working on a new routine." *Or something.* We don't ask questions about Grandmother's magical ways. She always returns with something new that changes the face of the show though, so we let her get away with being mysterious.

"Your grandmother can't just go running off whenever she feels like it." I don't have to see him to know his fists are clenched at his side. Samuel's reactions are as dependable as rain on the first night of the show in a new town.

Of course, my grandmother can do whatever she wants. She's responsible for three-fourths of the acts that perform in this tent. Samuel may own the place, but Grandmother is the one who keeps it running. If she wants to wander off to one of her many cabins along the route, no one is going to stop her—she comes back with magic every time she leaves and makes Samuel a ton of money.

"If she's not back by tomorrow, you're going after her." He's most definitely clenching.

"Mhmm," I murmur, pulling my legs back up from the sides to lift myself to face him again. He glares at me for a moment before looking around at the other's warming up under the enclosed tent.

"We don't have time for that!" Samuel shouts to them. "The people are here. We're starting early tonight! Places!"

I can hear one of my grandmother's many little sayings float through my mind. She's always coming up with strange things to say that make the most perfect sense…and then she uses them over and over as reminders to the crew.

Smoke for fire, she always says about Samuel. For as much as he tries to breathe flames, he's all talk.

Josephine's playing only slows for a moment as she registers his words, transitioning into the song she reserves for signaling the performers to hide from the incoming audience. We still have time before the people make their way to the tent, but many of us aren't allowed to be seen by the public until our appearance in the show, and have to get out of the main part of the tent.

Several of the men and women walk out of the tent to engage with the audience who has come to see the show before they take their seats inside the tent colored by yellow-tinted lights. I duck behind a curtain that separates the main ring from the area we've designated for the performers and walk toward my dressing room.

My trunk sits in the corner of my fabric-encased square room. There's enough space to change wardrobe and do my makeup. The walls of the tent don't block the sound, so Josephine's swelling music crashes through the backstage area loudly enough that it sounds like I'm in the center of the ring.

"Ready, Sienna?" Fannie's voice frightens me. I whip around to face the closed curtain that acts as a door.

"Almost," I answer, dipping my shoulder down as I slip the sleeve over my arm. The flesh-colored fabric settles snugly against my body, ribbon-like strips of red fabric wrapping around me dramatically to mesh with the silks as I perform. I loop the elastic over my finger to hold the sleeve in place, a sharp point dividing my hand in half.

The curtain moves as I push it open and step out in front of Fannie and Blanch. The two sparkle in deep purple tones adorned with silver accents. Both girls wear curled hair pinned back to the sides, the only difference in their ensembles is their hair color—Fannie a chestnut brown and Blanch the darkest raven-black I've ever seen. Grandma Ida did the girls a favor when she chose purple as their signature color.

"Trying to impress someone tonight?" Blanch muses, kicking her hip out to the side as she raises an eyebrow.

"No more than you are," I counter, releasing the curtain behind me.

A rush of wind passes by as Harriet rushes through with her batons. Had they been ablaze, she would have burned the tent down with the way she is moving.

"Slow down, Harriet, opening act isn't for another

two minutes!" Fannie calls after her playfully. The girl ignores her.

"One of these days she's going to turn around and breathe fire at you," I warn with a laugh.

"You mean I'd finally get a solo act?" Blanch grins. "I'm in."

She winks conspiratorially at me before turning to playfully yell, "Hey, Harriet!"

Fannie shoulders her friend like she does when one of the horses is being stubborn. Blanch holds her ground, barely swaying. Rolling my eyes, I push between the two toward the main part of the tent, ribbons in hand.

"Time to go, ladies."

Someone shifts the curtain concealing the backstage area from the main tent, allowing me to glance through it for just a moment. People file in, taking their seats as they wait for the show to begin. Josephine pounds out the notes on the organ, swelling enough to get the crowd ready for our grand entrance.

"I heard Ida still isn't back," Harriet murmurs, shifting anxiously next to me. She always arrives at the entrance before the rest of us, even though she's near the back of the lineup. "She's supposed to be changing my act when she gets back."

For a girl who works with fire for a living, she certainly is nervous before a performance. Working with fire may be the *only* time she's confident.

"If she's not back this evening, I'm being sent out to find her in the morning," I promise. She nods.

Suddenly, the music stops—our cue.

The lights on the other side of the curtain dim and the crowd falls silent. The lights go out completely, leaving us in the dark. Fabric rustles as Orville or one of the other boys whips open the curtain. As one, we rush into the ring and take our places, bathed in darkness.

Whispers fill the room from the audience as they wonder why it's taking so long without the lights on. Josephine presses one finger lightly on the organ key, followed slowly by another.

Deep breath.

Lights.

Roaring music crashes over the audience as the lights go on at full strength, drenching the ring in yellow. Throwing my hand up into the air, I release the ribbons. My face follows my initial move and I catch sight of rows of sparkling lights running from the center of the tent to the edges, mixed among chiffon fabric that matches my silks in an array of colors.

Looking back down, I see the crowd as the other performers start swirling around us. I dance with my ribbons, twirling them into the air to catch the attention of the onlookers. Most of us can't give our acts away yet, but the opening number still has to shock and awe the audience.

Fannie and Blanch find their horses across the tent and mount, standing on their saddles as they race around the outside of the ring. Ephraim juggles knives, concealing his true abilities for later.

Fire spins in the air as Harriet beams brightly, getting just close enough to the children to make their eyes grow wide. Orville leads in one of the elephants who circles the tent. Everyone glitters in the wardrobe picked by Grandma Ida for each individual person—no act has the same color or outfit design—we're all unique.

Red.

I'm only allowed to wear red when I perform. Grandma saved the color specifically for me. It was my mother's color before me and I inherited a different shade of it when I started my own act.

Blood. Fire. Intensity. Passion.

Grandmother always told me red was the color of war and strength, power and determination, desire, love, and passion. I love and loathe it all at the same time.

Grandma is a bit of a kingmaker. If the other circuses are to be listened to, she has the magic touch. Some even say she has real magic, but what she actually has is highly trained talent. Her skill at finding new acts is unparalleled. But even if Samuel brings in a new act, they have to pass Grandmother's tests to stay. Her word is final on a talent's success or removal from the show—she's always right. Samuel learned the hard way when he kept someone she turned down or dismissed someone grandma insisted we keep. With the way she always knows, it wouldn't surprise me if she was some magical creature sent to watch over us. If anyone in this world has *real* magic, it's Grandma Ida. I hope I've inherited some of that magic too.

My ribbons swirl around me as I move, contorting my body as I dance. Samuel stands in the center of the ring, eating up the attention in his black-and-white striped suit with accents of red and top hat, cane in hand, every bit a ringmaster.

The music grows as we finish our opening number. The crowd's gaze is fixed on the colorful spectacle. I run to the center of the ring, positioning myself—only a few notes left until all eyes will be on me.

The final notes.

I pass my ribbons off to Ephraim to carry out for me.

The lights go out.

Everyone else runs to clear the area. I remain, twirling the fabric one of the men lowers for me around my arms in my beginning pose, showing off the silks, one toe pointed gracefully in front of me.

A single light falls on me.

The group is transfixed by me as I start to move, leaving the fabric to fall behind me as I step forward, distracting them as the remaining performers leave the ring. Each step matches Josephine's music.

My costume matches the silks and once I'm in the air, it will look like it's part of the fabric, making me one with my apparatus.

I greet each section of the crowd, taking small bows or holding my arms out as I move around the center of the tent quickly before taking my place by the silks once more.

Lifting myself onto the silks is easy and I quickly climb high into the air—high enough to be seen by everyone without them having to struggle to look around the people in front of them. Just as I've been taught to do, I move into a double foot lock, wrapping the silks around my feet. Grandmother knew I needed to put on a show if I was to be the opening act for the circus and her routine never disappoints.

My wardrobe is overly hot in the sticky summer evening air, but it makes for a flashy show, which is exactly what Samuel demands of us. Twisting the silks behind my back, I drop into a cross back straddle, dangling my arms to the side high in the air, matching my outstretched legs. The children in the crowd gasp, shouting questions to their parents about why I'm hanging upside down.

I smile to myself as I move, twisting the silks counter-clockwise until I start spinning clockwise in the air. I've always loved the feeling of the lights dancing behind my eyelids as I close them just long enough to see the vibrant colors piercing through my makeup-covered eyelids. Opening my eyes, I reach up to right myself and climb higher as Josephine's music guides the viewers through my act's story.

The routine is only a few minutes long, but I've heard the audience say they were amazed by how it seemed I was up in the air for an eternity. I suppose to people who don't see it every day, it does seem like a rather long time. Samuel would never allow for a routine to last more than a few minutes though—he keeps us on a tight schedule, and we pack far too many acts into the show to dawdle. My body would be screaming if it were any longer, so I don't mind staying on task.

Nearing the end of my silks performance, I climb higher and make a show of wrapping the silks around my body. Inverting, I wrap one knee around the silks and grab the dangling end with my free hand. Looping it behind me, I wrap it around my lower leg. I twist my body around, positioning myself properly. The fabric wraps around my leg again, crossing in front of my body and around my back until it dangles freely again. With both hands, I clasp the fabric flowing beneath my head, knee still wrapped over the top part of the silks above me.

I take a breath to focus before straightening my leg and releasing my right hand straight out. My left hand guides the fabric as I finally allow myself to tip over, spinning into a triple star drop. I cascade down toward the ground, toppling over myself as part of the audience screams. The rest gasp.

My body stops, bouncing up slightly as the silks cushion me a few feet above the ground. My legs come together, pointing my toes as my hair sweeps the dirt. I only hold myself there for a moment before pulling myself upright. Using my legs, I spin myself, freeing my body of the final part of my wrap, then slide down the fabric to the ground.

The entire tent is silent. One breath. Two breaths. *Applause.*

I smile as Grandmother taught me to do, bowing to the corners of the tent. A little girl in the crowd catches my eye. She claps furiously, grinning at me.

Just then, the tent door rips back, revealing Blanch and Fannie. They ride in on their horses, a team of them in their wake. The two take turns leading their entrance, and the second rider always comes for me.

Still in my final pose, arms in the air, I wait until Blanch angles her horse at me at the last second. I run at full speed toward her, catching her wrist. I'm not sure how the girls manage to pull me onto their horse at a full gallop every night, but I hold on to them as we race around the ring.

Both girls slow their horses as we reach my exit,

allowing me to easily dismount before they rush to the center of the ring to perform.

"Nice work out there," Blanch calls before preparing to deposit me into the waiting arms of Orville.

"Thanks!" I yell before I fling myself off the horse's back, twirling in the air with a hand from Blanch. I land heavily against Orville's chest. He swings me, completing my motion and I fly through the partially open curtains into the backstage area.

I crash into Samuel and he makes sure I'm standing of my own accord before turning away, giving me a moment to stabilize myself. "Nice work out there, but you're still responsible for finding Ida in the morning. You were good, but not good enough to earn a morning off."

"Thanks, boss," I mutter under my breath as I push away from his chest and make my way back to my changing area to switch for my work on the lyra.

"Hey, Sienna," a deep voice says behind me. I don't have to turn.

"Hi, Elijah." My heart speeds up. I blame the triple star drop that was only supposed to be a double star drop.

Sometimes a girl likes to show off.

"That was impressive," he croons.

"It was supposed to be." *Confidence…I can pull this off.*

"It's nice to see a woman who knows what she's

doing." He peels off, fading into the crowd of people backstage.

"*Wow*," Ephraim says, sidling up next to me.

"Leave it alone, Eph." I roll my eyes.

"Fine, if that's what you want." He shrugs. "Do you want help tracking down Ida tomorrow, or should I leave that alone too?"

I've gone out numerous times to track down my grandmother on my own, but the majority of my friends protest. They don't like when I travel into unknown woods by myself. This town is particularly less high-end than where we normally travel, but Grandma Ida and my mother always taught me to be braver than I felt. Showing weakness never helped a female's case.

"I'll be fine. You get your beauty sleep," I quip. Glancing at him up and down from the corner of my eye, I add, "You need it."

"Fine," he jokes. "Be that way. But when you get kidnapped, don't expect me to come save you."

"Last time you thought I was going to fall down a pit and die, suddenly it's abduction?" I turned to face him as I walk. Spinning, I move backward. Ephraim reaches out to take my wrists, steadying me as I walk quickly backward. My hands rest on top of his, fingers tracing his forearm as I balance myself on my tiptoes to walk faster. We've always worked well together, even though we don't share an act.

"I'm just saying that I won't be the one to come and save you." He cocks an eyebrow.

"Elijah can come rescue me instead," I tease.

"Good luck with that," Ephraim mumbles. "He's more interested in the mirror than rescuing pretty girls."

"That's true." Harriet brushes past us, equipment in hand. We both pause to look at her before laughing.

"This is me," I say as we reach my dressing room curtain. I kick my leg out behind me for show, leaning onto his arms a touch. Ephraim bows his head slightly to say goodbye before leaving to get ready for his own act. It scares me when he has people attack him in the ring for show, but he always emerges unscathed.

"Wear something sparkly!" he shouts as he walks away.

"Always!"

While silks will always be my favorite apparatus, I love that working on the lyra gives me more freedom with my wardrobe. While everything has to be streamlined for silks so that nothing catches on the fabric, I can wear anything while working with my hoop.

"Sienna!" Ephraim pauses, glancing back. "Don't forget to wear something red when you sneak out early to look for Ida."

I wave him off and duck into my changing room.

Grandmother, though incredibly good at her job, is starting to lose her sight. She recognizes most people by their voice and their blurry signature color now. Wearing red helps her to identify me from a distance—I'll have to find something to wear since I can't take my wardrobe out of the circus without drawing too much attention and my jacket is ripped thanks to Hoyt and his tigers.

I'll figure it out later though—first I need to decide on my next show piece.

I rummage through my small trunk until I find the dress I want. Setting it over the top of the trunk, I turn to my small mirror and examine myself in my silks outfit before changing.

Strips of red fabric move over one shoulder and down my chest, wrapping around my waist. A second piece covers the other side of my chest, wrapping behind me. A large piece of red moves around my waist to swirl between my legs and around each thigh. It twists down around my knees, making me look like I'm wearing ballet slippers with incredibly wide ribbons tied around my calves.

While I have many different outfits, I wear this one when I'm feeling particularly bold. Mother never cared for it, but Grandmother said it made me look brave— perhaps I should wear *this* out to find Grandmother in the morning. In truth, this town makes me nervous and I don't like the idea of roaming around where I could run into anyone—best not to draw attention to myself.

What if I go out when I'm sure no one will be around?

The thought sparks in my head, making me duck as if I've been struck.

I *could* go out when no one was around. It would probably be safer. If I skip the end of the show and leave right after my next act, that will give me at least an hour to wander in the dark before the people start straying from inside the circus limits—likely two hours before the majority of them start to file away. It could be my best opportunity to avoid the townspeople.

I tug down the sleeve of my outfit, sliding it to the floor. Noise fills the area outside of my dressing room and I quickly hurry into my next outfit. The translucent skirt drops to the floor in front of me, slits all the way up to my waist. The bodice wraps similarly to my last outfit, coming to a point in the middle in various shades of sparkling red. Behind me, I clasp the high collar, adjusting the feathers off of my right shoulder. I consider leaving the detached sleeves off for the evening, but they really *do* complete the outfit—we all have to suffer for our beauty in this heat.

Tying my curls back into a high ponytail, I give myself at least a little grace when it comes to dealing with the sweltering heat. The tent makes everything so much hotter with all the people in it. Perhaps I'll leave my hair up when I slip out later.

Stepping out of my changing area, I look for Samuel to tell him I'll be leaving tonight. He doesn't do well when Grandmother isn't around to oversee his circus, so I'm sure he won't mind if I skip the closing number to retrieve her from the woods. I'll have to find out if she took anyone with her or not—Grandmother likes to disappear without telling anyone she's going, occasionally taking a performer or two with her for training.

Before I can take more than three steps, Fannie has me cornered. After she gives me the full rundown of their part of the show, I mention I'll be slipping out early so they can cover for me in the finale. Blanch nods but looks worried, as does Fannie. They know better than to argue.

I find Samuel, explain what I'll be doing, and get his approval before making my way to the ring to wait for my next call time. My lyra performance goes quickly enough and I block out Samuel's instructions to return immediately to the tent with Grandmother this evening. He almost sounded worried for my safety...*almost*.

I change into all black, wearing pants and a fitted top with a belt to the side to hold my knife, water, and a few extra things I carry with me when I go out. Without a jacket to wrap myself in, my only option is my red cloak. Once my boots are tied, I pull the cloak around my shoulders and step out into the night air, leaving the hood off. Not wanting to deal with the warmth of the fabric, I push it off of my arms, behind my shoulder, leaving it to hang from my neck. It's uncomfortable but not as bad as the sweltering heat.

Stars glisten in the sky as the crickets shriek their high-pitched songs. Darkness surrounds me, leaving only the faint glow of the lights outside the tent to cast my long shadow over the dark grass. The noise from the tent silences in my wake as I walk away, and I pray everyone remains at the circus and not prowling around in the dark.

Ephraim was wrong—I don't need to be more worried about the world. I'm already terrified of it.

The noise I hear next gives me good reason to be.

A MAN GROWLS BEHIND ME. I SPIN, READY TO DEFEND myself.

"Did clearing my throat scare you?" Elijah grins arrogantly at me.

"Don't you have a show to do?"

"Do I?" he questions. Elijah takes a step toward me.

"You're supposed to," I challenge, crossing my arms. The wind kicks up at just the right moment, making my cloak shift behind me. If only Grandmother could see me now—she'd be so proud of my wardrobe-moment.

"I'm going with you," he replies. "The woods are no place for a woman this time of night."

"Everyone is here at the show. I'll be fine," I counter.

"You want me to stay and deprive you of my company?" he asks. "I hardly think so. I promise, I won't make your boyfriend jealous."

"Boyfriend?"

"The *invincible* one…"

I reach up to tuck my hair behind my ear. "Just friends."

"I know." Elijah grins. "That's been made *very* clear; I just like testing the waters."

The new act is a troublemaker.

"Perceptive."

"I'm aware of many things, Sienna." Elijah runs his hand through his hair as he steps toward me. "Shall we?"

"If you want to test Samuel's wrath, be my guest." I motion for him to walk with me. Turning, I lead the way, pretending I know where I'm going.

We walk in silence until the glow of the circus lights is completely in the distance. The moon's glow illuminates our path, brightly reflecting the hidden sun.

"The last circus I worked in wasn't as brightly colored." Elijah makes small talk. "They focused on a black and white scheme."

"Sounds macabre," I muse.

Elijah's hands are clasped behind his back as we walk and I fight not to mimic him. Grandmother taught me not to copy others—it suggests that they are the leader and we are the followers. I hold my hands at my side, tucked just behind my cape as it billows out behind me.

"Why are you wearing that?" He nods to my cloak.

"So that Grandmother Ida can see me. She can't always make out faces from a distance, but colors help."

"I've heard she has magic—real magic. That's what all the other circuses are saying. I'm surprised she can't just heal herself so she can see again."

People have been claiming Grandmother was magic for the majority of my life. She took a small circus and transformed it into one of the best-known shows in the country in a matter of months. She teaches our people to do things no other circus can pull off. In truth, I think she enjoys being mysterious about it—she plays into what people say about her. I've believed it a time or two myself —how else can I explain some of the things she's capable of?

"Why red?" Elijah asks before I can respond.

Stepping out of the field and into the woods, the fallen leaves start to crunch under our feet despite it being the middle of summer. The trees are far less dense than many of the woods I've been in, allowing the moonlight to easily pass through to us.

"It's a family color."

"Ida doesn't wear red," he points out.

"That's a story for another time," I interject. I don't feel like talking about my mother right now or why Ida doesn't dress like me anymore. "How are you finding the circus?"

"I'm settling in," he drawls, hands in his pockets.

"I've seen your act a few times," I mention. "You're pretty good."

"I was trained by the best." His words come quickly and easily.

"Yet, you left…"

The breeze picks up slightly, rustling the leaves in the trees. My hair brushes across my face from behind, tickling my cheekbones and chin.

"I went out on my own. You can't be an apprentice forever, Sienna."

"But you're willing to throw it away to walk into the woods in the dark of night," I point out.

"Protecting one of Samuel's star acts hardly seems like an offense." He glances at me from the corner of his eye, barely turning to acknowledge me. "He'll get over it. Besides, it's only been two months—I'm hardly of value yet—and the closing number is just showing off. There's no real magic in it."

"I'd still be afraid of getting in trouble."

"You're afraid of a lot, aren't you, Red Girl?" He uses the nickname some of the other performers call me. We all have one, but I've been here longer than most and my color stuck.

"No," I lie. If only Ephraim could hear this conversation. "I'm out in the woods alone at night—do I seem like a coward to you?"

"You seem stupid." He pauses, realizing he insulted me. "Going out in the dark in a strange town isn't safe. You shouldn't just go out on impulse."

"Didn't you just tell me I was timid?"

"You can be timid and still make poor decisions, Sienna. You need to be careful whom and what you trust. Putting your faith in a fabric tent to keep people in while you wander out alone is hardly a wise choice."

"I didn't see you stop me."

The trees open back up into a small clearing of tall grass. I don't like walking where I can't see, and there's very likely ticks and other creatures in there, but Elijah doesn't hesitate, so neither do I. The grass tickles my elbows as I hold my hands up out of the way—at least my pants will protect my legs, but my arms are bare.

The earrings I put on before I left dangle around my chin. Every few steps, one swings into my line of sight, catching the light from the moon. I walk more intentionally in order to swing them more, the light soothing me and giving me something to focus on as we walk through the tall grass. Something scurries away from us in the dark and I fight to control my breathing.

"Where are we looking?" Elijah asks, changing the subject.

"I don't know. Ida goes where she pleases. I'm not sure if she took anyone with her this time to train." I speed up to keep step with Elijah. "Honestly, I thought she might have taken *you* out here. You were gone when she slipped off, but I saw you the next day. I heard she might have found some new talent, but I'm not sure. It's always a guessing game with Grandma Ida."

He chuckles. "Keeping tabs on me?"

I laugh, trying to play it off. "I notice everything."

"Did you notice me noticing you?" His pace slows, as does everything in my world.

"No," I reply cautiously. "I didn't notice that."

"Maybe you haven't been watching carefully enough." He laughs quietly again. "Magicians like being watched closely, Sienna. You're hurting my feelings."

He's definitely trouble.

"Is there some way for you to know where Ida went or are we going to be wandering around all night?"

I shake my head, clearing my thoughts.

"Usually she leaves me some markers." My eyes start sweeping from tree to tree as we step back out of the small clearing. "I'm the only one that can spot them though."

"Ah, a secret. I can back that."

"You like secrets?" I ask, absentmindedly as I start to look for Grandmother's signals to me.

"Secrets are the fuel the world runs on, Sienna. The more secrets you have, the more power you hold."

In the bush, I see the mark my grandmother has left for me—three broken branches in a row, all bending down toward the ground, even though they've been snapped at a sideways angle.

"This way," I mutter, pulling us off to the left.

Elijah raises an eyebrow at me but doesn't ask how I know.

He's not supposed to know how we communicate, so I try to distract him.

"How long have you been performing magic?"

"A few years." He takes his left hand out of his pocket and loops it through his belt loop, allowing it to dangle next to me. My companion steps to the side just enough to shift closer to me. A few more shifts and he will be touching my arm. "A few different shows tried to poach me over the years, but I was loyal. Once he felt I was ready, my teacher sent me out to find my own work."

"Which is why you joined us."

"No, I was with another circus first, but they didn't have what I was looking for, so I moved on after a time."

"Are you finding that here, or will you be leaving us too?"

Elijah pauses for a moment, not answering. When he finally speaks, he says, "I think I might have found what I've been looking for." He waits again. "I'm very interested to meet your grandmother. We've talked a little, but I haven't been able to see any of that magical wisdom she's become known for."

"I'm sure you'll get a chance when we find her."

"Samuel seems very anxious to find her."

"He is." I step around an exposed root, nearly catching

my toe on a rock instead. "Perhaps you could teach me to do a few simple magic tricks sometime. We haven't had a magician in the show for years, but I was always mesmerized by sleight-of-hand when I was younger."

"Are you trying to get me up on your silks, madam? Because that won't happen. Unlike your friend, I have no use for spending time in the air."

"I wasn't proposing a trade unless you wanted one."

"But you will offer *something* in exchange for my time and knowledge…"

"The pleasure of my company, good sir," I quip. I spot Grandmother's signal again and keep us to the left once more.

"A fair trade, then, I see." He nods. A small smile tugs on his lips.

"Babur!" a yell pierces the otherwise quiet night. I whip around.

"What is it?" Elijah asks, turning with me.

"Babur?" a second, less-certain voice takes up the cry.

"Orville?" I yell.

Silence hangs between us for a moment.

"Sienna?"

"Here," I call back, walking toward the sound of his voice.

"Careful, Babur is loose." He crashes through the trees until I can see him. Hoyt follows behind him, chain in hand.

"Babur is…?" Elijah asks uneasily.

"Tiger," I respond. Orville approaches, taking my outstretched hands in his. He ducks, looking into my eyes in the moonlight.

"Babur escaped, we don't know how, but we have to find him before the show gets out." He glances at Elijah. "Let's split up. Elijah, go with Hoyt."

He tugs on my hand as Elijah protests.

"He's right," I interject. "Hoyt trained Babur—you're safe with him. Orville works with the elephants and has more experience with animals than either of us. We'll have to find Ida tomorrow—this is more important. We need to get Babur home before the townspeople notice him wandering and try to hurt him."

A strange expression flashes on Elijah's face—I can't tell if he's relieved or upset. After a moment, he nods, accepting the arrangement. Without another word, we split.

"How could this have happened?" I mutter to Orville.

"There was no damage to the cage. It looks like someone let him out." His words hit me with the same force the ground does when I occasionally slip off the lyra in practice when I'm not paying attention. "Babur!"

I listen through the darkness and trees, hoping to detect the sound of a tiger's paws. Nothing.

"What do we do if we can't find him?"

"Tell the town. Likely get run out."

"We have to find Ida before we get run out. I just hope we find Babur before the townspeople do."

"We will. He can't have gone far—he never strays from Hoyt for too long. The guy practically raised him since he was a cub."

"Are you saying Hoyt is his mother?" I snicker at the image of Hoyt as the compassionate, caring type.

"Something like that." Orville grins. He runs a hand through his long, blond hair. If their faces weren't different enough, I'd say he and Ephraim could be brothers, but cousins is close enough. "Nice cape, by the way."

"Hoyt ruined my jacket last week; it's all I had."

"No luck finding Ida then, I take it?" We duck under a tree branch.

"Clearly didn't get that far."

"Babur!" Orville suddenly shouts, interrupting my final word. Turning back to me, he adds, "Did you really think it was wise to come out at night?"

"I thought everyone would be in the tent for another hour and I'd have time."

Just as we step out of the trees and into the clearing, something rushes at us. It tramples through the grass, nearly colliding with Orville.

"We found him!" Elijah gasps. "Come help."

CHAPTER THREE

"YOU CORRALLED A TIGER?" BLANCH ASKS IN DISBELIEF.

"That's not the important question here!" Fannie practically shouts, turning on Blanch. "She was surrounded by three of the most gorgeous men in this circus and you're worried about a *cat?*" Fannie protests.

"We *really* need to realign your priorities, Fannie." Blanch glares at her shaking her head in mock disbelief.

"A tiger, huh?" Ephraim interrupts. Fannie and Blanch beam at him. "I knew you wanted to expand your act, Sienna, but a tiger? Are you going to start getting a big head too like the other trainers?"

He sits down next to us on the edges of the benches that we moved to the side of the food tent.

"Hoyt's been looking for a new partner, I hear." Fannie bats her eyelashes at Ephraim.

He leans forward, placing his elbows on his knees. "Well," he drops his voice conspiratorially, "if *you* switch to work with Hoyt, Fannie, I'll be available to work with Blanch."

He swings around to face the raven-haired girl. Blanch laughs, leaving Fannie shocked for a moment before she laughs too. Ephraim has endured Fannie's flirtatious side for years and enjoys teasing her back.

"I accept," Blanch finally struggles to say. "Lose the shirt and we're good to go. Training begins tomorrow."

Ephraim's grin grows as his eyebrows shoot up. Reaching for his collar, he begins to unbutton his shirt, pretending to leer at our friend. I laugh and swat at his arm. He sways sideways a little with my strike, fixing the top button.

"Are you going to let me accompany you today, Sienna? Since you have such a tendency to find vicious creatures out there." His grin turns into a sincere smile as he looks over to me.

"You'd better not be calling my tigers *vicious*, Ephraim." Hoyt sits down next to us, balancing a plate of food on his knee.

"I was actually referring to the wolf who followed her out into the dark." Ephraim shoots an icy glance at Elijah across the tent.

"There's something off about him," Hoyt agrees.

"You mean the fact that he's gorgeous?" Fannie counters.

"Who's gorgeous?" Josephine sits down with us.

"Elijah."

Josephine's eyes grow wide. She's usually fantastic at schooling her long, oval-shaped face into compliance, keeping us from reading her expression, but not this morning. Her gentle features spark to life as she glances down.

"My point exactly." Fannie crosses her arms triumphantly.

"Yes," Blanch replies, also crossing her arms at her friend. "But his attention isn't on *you,* is it?"

"I'm willing to share the attention with Sienna for now," Fannie says benevolently.

"Back to the point," Ephraim redirects us. He points to the group. "Can we walk you, Sienna?"

"You know Ida doesn't like big productions," I reply. Everyone looks at me.

"You realize where we are, right?" Orville points out from his place by his cousin. "This thing is called a tent. It's similar to the big one we perform under *every night* for *thousands of people.*"

I roll my eyes at him.

"I don't need a keeper, thank you."

"At least take *one* of us with you," Ephraim pleads. "A few of the townspeople saw you bringing Babur back last night—I'm sure word has gotten around by now."

"Which means they'll be looking for a tiger, not a girl."

"Which means they'll be in the woods *looking*." Orville jumps in before Ephraim can argue.

"Take someone, Sienna," Hoyt encourages. He grins viciously at me. "*I* volunteer."

"Yeah, go with Hoyt; I'll keep Elijah company while you're gone." Fannie smiles brilliantly at me, bobbing her head from side to side as if she won.

"I'll go." Harriet sits down with us, her long, dark hair free from the bun she wears it in while performing. One dark finger points back to herself. "After all, I'm the one who works with fire every night. The only one who does more dangerous work is Clarence."

Ephraim looks affronted. "You think the man getting shot out of a cannon into a net has a more dangerous job than the man who gets punched in the gut by a strongman every night?"

"*Nobody* could get past *those* abs, darling." We all turn to Blanch, shocked that wasn't Fannie's answer. "Oh. I need to stop spending so much time with my partner. I'm so sorry." Blanch looks horrified that she spoke.

All of the men look quite pleased with her outburst. Ephraim's eyes sparkle. "Thank you, Blanch."

"I'm still going to be more helpful to Sienna than *you* lot." Harriet declares. "Samuel isn't going to fare well if we don't get Ida back soon."

She sits back as her nervous side comes out. Whenever she's anxious, her bravado fades.

"I'll be fine," I protest. "It's light out; nothing is going to happen."

I refuse to look at Ephraim, but I can feel his eyes on me.

"Let her go," Josephine's quiet voice stops everyone. "She's done this before. She does it all the time when Ida wanders away to work. We're better off here doing damage control from Babur's unplanned walk last night. We need to show them that it's business as usual and no one here is worried that another tiger might escape."

She doesn't say it, but she also means they need to figure out who let the tiger out in the first place.

"I can take Caleo for a walk," Orville suggests. "She hasn't had a good walk since we arrived the other day, aside from running around the ring."

"Good, take the elephant for a walk," Josephine directs.

"Someone want to help with Brisheet?"

I stand as they debate what they should do to maintain appearances around the tents. I make it to the exit before Ephraim catches up to me.

"Be safe," he says quietly into my ear as he leans in behind me. Ephraim presses a knife into my hand. I tuck it into my belt that sits over my long, gray skirt.

He brushes away from me, not waiting for an answer.

The circus is a different place in the daylight. Outside of the colorful tent, everything is bathed in white light from the sun. The circus lights won't be on for hours and I miss the colorful glow of red, blue, green, and yellow from the bulbs strung across the tents.

It's not nearly as warm as it was last night, but it's still early morning; there's time for it to warm up more. The noise from the animals mixes with performers calling to one another. Many of the men are working on projects, building new set pieces, repairing damage from the night before, or moving feed for the animals. I slip past them quietly.

Thinking twice, I move the knife Ephraim handed me to my boot, just in case. I check the knife that was already sitting on my hip to ensure I can remove it easily should I need to use it, and then I set out away from the circus perimeter.

Having already discovered part of the path last night, it's easier to get on the right track today. I quickly locate the broken branches and make my way along the path. The birds escort me as I walk.

Unfortunately, the tall grass is just as concerning as it was last night now that I can see the spiders everywhere. I go out of my way to walk around the area.

I make it several more markers before I notice the noise behind me. At first, I think it's the wind in the trees and bushes, but as the noise persists, I convince myself that I'm not alone.

My hand automatically reaches for the knife at my hip.

"Planning to cut my heart out?" A familiar voice asks. I relax as Elijah steps into sight.

"Sneaking up on women in the woods isn't encouraged, Elijah," I remind him.

"You knew I was here."

My eyes involuntarily sweep the length of him taking in his dark clothing. In return, he slowly looks me over.

"Shall we?" Elijah holds out a hand, pointing away from where I'm walking. Without waiting, he takes several long strides toward me, grabs my elbow, turning me, and propels me forward in the direction of his choosing—the wrong way.

"We shall." I pull my elbow away. "But we're going *this* way."

I wonder if he's going to argue for a moment. He pulls out a few cut ropes instead. Holding them up, he shows me the three different lengths.

"Let's make a wager. If you can turn these ropes into three matching ropes of the same length, we'll go your way. If you can't, we go my way."

A smile tugs at my lips as I indulge his game. This might prove interesting.

With a big flourish, he shows off each rope he's holding in his left hand. Elijah draws out the process, talking about each one in great detail as he loops the ends up into his waiting fingers. Once he's displayed each of the three ropes, he grabs onto three ends and pulls. Each of the three ropes has transformed into the same length —a trick that would shock anyone.

The magician grins flirtatiously at me, then crumples the ropes into the palm of his hand. Pulling them out one at a time, he reveals three vastly different lengths of rope. Raising an eyebrow, he hands them to me to inspect.

I tug on each, ensuring that they are solid pieces of rope. Nothing has been cut, there's nothing sneaky about them. The trick is pure magic.

What Elijah doesn't know is that I also know how to perform this trick. I might not know much about magic, but I know enough to get by if I ever need to entertain a group of people. Our last magician taught me this one.

Placing the ropes in my hand, I pretend to mimic him. I let my voice waver just enough as I'm repeating his words to make him think I'm uneasy. Each rope is held out in my hand, displaying the length before tucking them up to create the loops just as Elijah had. At just the right moment, I dart my eyes away to something behind him. Just as I knew he would, he tracks my movements.

As he glances back, I take a deep, steadying breath. Repeating everything he said, I pull the ropes down, revealing the same length ropes dangling from my hand. His jaw drops.

After a moment, he meets my eyes and grins. "Well played."

I swirl my hand over the ropes, moving differently than he did to reveal the ropes returned to their natural, uneven state. Elijah reaches out for his ropes. I place them in his hand, and he tucks them away. I spin before he has a chance to protest.

"Nice of you to join me again," I comment, cloak billowing out behind me with my quick steps.

"You still shouldn't be out here alone."

"Don't pretend you're here for me. We both know you're here to see Ida."

His footsteps suddenly stop behind me. I walk a few more feet before turning around.

"What if I'm here for *you*?"

A single rose made out of lace fabric rests high on his left lapel, just below his shoulder. From it, three silver chains so dark they're almost black dangle across to his right side, halfway between his hip and shoulder. They sparkle in the sunlight dancing through the swaying trees.

Elijah's jacket is long, resting over a brocade fabric vest in a steely gray color that's nearly black as well. Black boots stick out under tight, black pants, completing his look. He's left his gloves at the circus, apparently, or tucked into one of his many hidden pockets. He looks every bit a renowned magician, even if he's only been in the public eye for a few months with Samuel's crew.

"Perhaps I'm here for both." He takes my silence as an accusation.

His strides are long once more as he moves toward me. Just as I think he's about to bury his hand in my hair, he moves, tipping my chin up to him. His other hand grabs my waist roughly, pulling me toward him.

"Is that really such a bad thing?" he murmurs inches from my lips.

Elijah pulls away, moving around me. Stunned, I don't move for a moment. I nearly contort myself around without taking the time to turn my feet to see his reaction.

"I imagine it is." I finally turn, stalking toward him. "I'll forgive you *this* time, but—"

His lips silence me. This time, he tugs on my hair, opening my face to his. One hand slips low on my back, making me shudder. I did exactly what he wanted.

Elijah slams me against a tree a few feet away, kissing me the entire time. My fingers run over the chains on his chest until I reach his shoulder. I've never been kissed like this before, but I quickly learn that I don't mind it.

I brush over his ear, pinning it to the side of his head as I work my fingertips into his dark hair. Elijah's high cheekbones are sharp against my skin as he moves to the spot just below my ear, making me gasp.

It's only a moment before we pull away, but it feels like something has changed. I look down at the forest floor and focus on the crumbling leaves that are attempting to cling to their last bit of life now that they've fallen.

"I want to know everything about you," he murmurs. I giggle; I can't help it.

"I'd like to know about you too, Elijah."

"You first." He sounds breathless as he pulls away, leaving me resting against the tree. I force myself to push away from it, testing my legs gently to make sure I won't fall on my newly-weakened knees.

When I'm sure I can walk, I join him, letting him guide our path for a few minutes as I search for the next marker. Thankfully, he continues in the direction I had set us on before his interruption.

"How long have you been with Samuel's circus?"

"My entire life," I answer. The birds seem extra happy today as they sing to us. "I grew up there. Ida has been with Samuel since the beginning and my family has always stayed."

"When can I meet the rest of your family?"

"It's just me and Ida now." I try to keep the emotion out of my voice.

He makes a small noise and nods.

"You and Ida seem to be doing well for yourselves. Have you ever considered working anywhere else? You might be paid better elsewhere, especially with both of your talents."

"Oh, we'd never leave. As rough as he is, Samuel is family, and so are the others. Besides, Samuel would be lost without Grandmother."

"I can believe that—it certainly seems like Ida does a lot there."

"She does. She's been training me to take over for her, and it turns out that she does *so much more* than I thought. I don't think anyone is really aware of just how much Grandmother does to organize and run that show."

"It's nice that she's letting you take over," he says casually. "How much are you doing now?"

"Can you keep a secret?"

He perks up as I transition into being conspiratorial. "I'm a magician; what do you think?"

"Good point—you're probably the best of us all at keeping secrets." I pause for effect. "Grandmother has been training me for a while now. She's stepped back quite a bit. I don't know it *all* yet—and *Samuel* has no idea —but she's been letting me make most of the decisions and then she communicates them to the team. She wants it to be a seamless transition one day, even though she's not ready to retire and just come along for the ride yet."

"Samuel's going to let her retire?"

"No." I laugh. "That's why we're doing it this way. He will never know I've taken over until it's just me completely handling everything and Ida shows him proof that I can handle it."

"Will you be taken off your act at that point?" Concern hitches his voice slightly.

"I'm not going anywhere." I bump his hand with the back of mine. "I might transition some of my duties. If I really need to, we can find a second aerialist act to work with me and alleviate some of my duties, but only if we need to. I'll begin training people at some point over the next year or two, as well."

"So, you'll be disappearing on these little trips too?"

Elijah is good at putting the pieces together. I suppose I'll have to start making some disappearing trips of my own so people don't put it together when Ida and I both disappear all the time.

"Any chance you'll need company? Magicians are pretty good at disappearing acts—I could help."

He grins without looking at me. I tear my eyes away as we split to walk around a tree in our path, each taking a side. When we converge, he takes my hand, holding it tightly.

"I have a confession." Elijah's words are rushed.

Is he nervous?

"We need to go this way." He points. Before I can protest, he continues, gripping my hand tighter as if I might run away. "I've been working with Ida. I wasn't supposed to tell anyone. We've been trying something."

What?

Grandmother never tells me who she's bringing out into the woods to test new acts with, but I never would have guessed that she'd bring Elijah out so early—especially since he was still with us for most of her time away. She usually waits several months for new performers to establish themselves before she helps refine their act…and to make sure they stick around that long.

"She's not over there anymore—she left last night. We had to move for what we were working on."

"What are you working on?" I start to pull away. He holds me in place.

"Magic. *Real* magic."

"Real magic doesn't exist, Elijah. It's all sleight-of-hand and trickery. We make them believe, but there's logic behind it all."

Right? Something ticks inside my brain. If *anyone* had access to *real* magic, it would be Grandmother. But surely, she doesn't…

"Not in this case. We've discovered something. You'll see. Come on."

He pulls me along behind him. It takes a moment while I'm processing his words, but I catch up to him.

"You're sure this is the way?" I ask after a few minutes of him explaining why he didn't tell me he had been working with Ida again, reiterating the same thing in four different ways without giving me any additional information.

That's when I hear her voice. It's a quick shout in the distance. Before I can run to Grandmother, Elijah drops my hand, flinging his arm in front of me to stop me from rushing forward.

"It's part of it!"

"What's happening?" I struggle to get around him.

Spinning, he faces me, using both arms to pin mine against my body. Elijah puts a foot behind him to brace himself as he pushes against me to counter my momentum. Neither of us are able to break the force of the other, pinning us to our place in the middle of the forest.

"Sienna, you can't go over there, it's part of the process." He glances back over his shoulder, struggling against me.

"What is happening?" I demand as her next shout is cut off. I scream around Elijah since I can't move past him. "*Grandmother?*"

Everything goes silent but Elijah.

"You…can't—" His words are separated as he tries to counter my movements. An angry male voice cuts him off.

"What is this?"

My blood runs cold as I make eye contact.

CHAPTER FOUR

"Ida, I had to tell her." Elijah cuts me off. He refuses to release his grip on my upper arms.

Throwing my left elbow up between us, I bring it down on his forearm and break his hold. Twisting, I wrench my right side away from him. He holds his hands out at me as if he had just encountered one of Hoyt's tigers and was trying to tame it with his words.

"I'm sorry, Ida," he addresses the man again. "I had to tell your granddaughter about the new act we were working on." He turns back to me. "Sienna, I'm sorry I couldn't tell you before. I knew it would be hard to believe and you'd have to see the transformation for yourself."

He glances at the man again. His dirty blond hair is stringy, falling past his shoulders. His brows are dark and far thicker than the bit of facial hair that surrounds his lips and chin. The man glares at me as Elijah continues.

"Ida"—he turns and nods at the man—"and I have been working on transformation magic. It's your grandmother."

He looks desperately at me before turning back to the man. Elijah walks quickly to his side, the man's gaze fixed on him. The man's eyebrows furrow, but he quickly raises them, nodding.

"Hello, my dear," the man addresses me.

Elijah turns, reaching out to me, waving me over. "Come."

I blink. There's no way the man in front of me is my grandmother. She's a woman and two generations older than the man in front of me.

They can tell I don't believe them. The man steps away from Elijah. Reaching down, he pauses until he's sure I'm watching. He snaps one, two, three branches right next to each other—Ida's signal that I'm moving in the right direction.

"Grandmother?" I ask in disbelief. He nods.

"We've been working on this for a while now, Sienna," Elijah supplies. "It's why Ida brought me into the show—I have a gift and so does she—even more than me. We weren't sure we had it right, but she insisted on trying it before she would let any of us test it. We're planning on using it as part of my act originally, but then we're going to expand it to several of the other acts as well.

"I know you're *taking over for your grandmother*," he

glances at the person next to him, "but we wanted to make sure we had this right before we told you in case it failed—we didn't want this bit of it coming back on you if it didn't work. Your grandmother wants you to succeed in taking over for her and she knew you'd push this once you knew about it, even if it failed. She didn't want you constantly working to make a failure succeed. But it's worked, Sienna! It's worked!"

The man beside Elijah watches him carefully, nodding slowly, then faster before turning to look at me.

"What is this?" I ask skeptically, locking eyes with my...*grandmother*.

"Magic, dear. I knew Elijah would be the one to help us figure it out." The voice is dark and low. Even if Grandmother had transformed herself somehow, I can't imagine this is what she would sound like posing as a man.

"How are you doing this? Even if you *could* change your appearance, how are you getting your voice to do that?"

When did I start believing this man is my grandmother?

"Come, I'll explain everything." Grandmother motions to me, her fingers now long and gnarled much differently than her aged skin. "But I need to *show* you. It's not just magical words, my dear. It's so much more."

"And it requires a great deal of additional space, which is why we moved," Elijah interjects, earning a glare from Grandmother—something I'm well accustomed to.

I take a cautious step toward them. Elijah takes his place by Grandmother and elbows her slightly—I don't think I was supposed to notice.

"It may be hard to see you, dear, but even *I* can tell you're hesitating. Come along now."

I feel like I've been struck. It *has* to be her, right? If she still can't see, that means even though her appearance has changed, she's still in there.

"Come, come." *Impatience.* Perhaps it *is* her.

Lifting my skirt, I follow. What choice do I have? If Grandmother has discovered something, I need to learn what it is.

"Why were you shouting?" I ask, standing alongside them as they begin to walk.

"The transformation process," Elijah jumps in. "It's a bit painful at first, but it seems to be getting easier."

"How many times have you done this?" I ask in horror, looking at my grandmother posing as someone else. She looks far too dark for the Grandmother I know.

"A few." I wonder if she means to sound like she's grumbling or if it's a byproduct of the transformation process.

"Can you change back now?"

They both turn to look at me.

"No. It's not possible because—"

"No, the effects last for several hours at a time." Elijah quickly supplies. "Ida *just* changed, so she'll be like this for a bit. Don't worry, it will make traveling easier, won't it, Ida?"

Grandmother nods.

"You're still unsure," Elijah sounds disappointed. He looks to the man next to him.

The man reaches into his pocket and pulls out a red ribbon crossed over itself in a loop with a point where the ribbons meet. Grandmother has worn it on her left wrist under her sleeve since the first day I started training on silks.

It's her. There's no doubt in my mind that this is her.

The man—*Grandmother*—smiles at me. Tucking it back into the pocket it came out of, my grandmother nods at me.

"This way, children." Grandmother has always called everyone *child*. It's a term of endearment, but also a reminder of who is in charge. Even Samuel has to endure it.

Grandmother leads the way, clad in her signature dark clothing. I wonder if her outfit changed in the transformation process or if she had donned those clothes before it began. I've heard rumors about another circus having the power to change a person's being, but until this moment, I thought they were only rumors sent out by the ringmaster himself to try to drum up more business and downplay Ida's renown—very few circuses get the attention Samuel's show gets.

Elijah takes a place next to me, allowing me to walk just slightly ahead of him. Grandmother's new strides are long—even longer than Elijah's—and I have to hurry to keep pace. We move so fast that I can barely keep track of where we're going.

I try to ask questions along the way, but they both keep telling me they just have to show me. After twenty minutes, we reach the edge of a clearing that could have also been a fantastic place for Samuel to set the tent up.

Past that, there's nothing but more trees and small clearings. I give up asking questions and let them lead me further away. Birds chatter in the distance. Once in a while, a pair of squirrels will chase each other across our path.

"We're close," Elijah informs me, taking my hand surreptitiously. He drops his voice to a whisper. "No matter what you see, just stay by me and hold my hand."

Fear pricks the back of my neck. The light streams through the trees ahead, suggesting we're about to walk out of the forest and into the open. Despite the summer heat, everything feels cold.

I balk.

Elijah turns to look at me, tugging on my hand. There's fear in his eyes, pulling slightly at the corners just enough to make him look concerned. "You have to come."

I don't. I stay rooted to the ground as he pulls harder on me.

"Come along," Grandmother says matter-of-factly. "We don't have time for this."

"It will be fine. Can you trust me?" Elijah asks, changing his demeanor. He's no longer trying to be forceful, but his words from before have a lasting impact.

Grandmother moves forward, not waiting.

I take a tiny step forward.

"See?" Elijah asks. "I'll be right here with you."

Slowly, I let him guide me to the clearing. Across a cut-down meadow, there's a caravan of wagons and small tents—another circus traveling through.

"What is this?" I demand. Whatever this is, it isn't right.

"Come along," Grandmother insists again. "We haven't time for this."

Her outfit is similar to Elijah's but far less showy. It's dark-colored with a long jacket that sways around the knees. Tall boots sit over long trousers. A billowy shirt peeks out from under the jacket—it's not a show piece.

"It's a circus," Elijah whispers. "Just come inside and see."

A large tent is set up similar to our food tent. It's large enough to hold the crew of a circus, but not big enough to perform in. The fabric is dark, just like both of my companion's outfits.

There are enough animals around to hear and smell from the tent, even though I can't see them. Glancing around, I note a number of cages laying about, though none of them appear to be homes to animals—they're far too pristine. Chains sit on the ground, forcing us to maneuver around them.

The tent is relatively empty save for a few performers dressed in black and white wardrobe. Their lines are sharp and piercing, highlighted by the commanding contrast of their colors. They look over to us pointedly and wait.

"This is that aerialist I was telling you about," Grandmother addresses the group. "She'll be joining us today."

A man and a woman painted nearly white with pink makeup around their eyes look at me in shock. A third who looks to be some sort of court jester from books looks at me with a reaction I could almost classify as pity, though it's hard to tell with the strange makeup on. The rest simply nod and look away.

"Sit," Grandmother commands.

"Are you hungry?" Elijah asks. He's still holding my hand tightly. I shake my head no.

Elijah sits beside me. Grandmother walks away toward the small crowd of performers.

"Where are we?" I whisper.

"Ida just needs to talk to some people first and then we'll explain." He pats my hand with his free one.

After a moment, Ida walks back, and I hope she transforms back to herself soon. It's disconcerting to be staring at her in the form of a younger man like this.

Grandmother steps forward, looming over me. I didn't realize how tall she was in this form. I nearly stand up, but something in Grandmother's expression tells me not to move.

"I'm going to show you something." Grandmother holds her hand out to me. "It will wear off soon and I need to show you before it does."

Elijah quietly nods next to me. I take Grandmother's hand and rise. We leave the tent and the strange performers behind.

The sun is high overhead, making the heat unbearable again. I wonder if I can take the cloak off since Grandmother knows I'm here now, but I dare not ask as we walk.

Stepping into another tent, Grandmother adds, "We perform closer magic here. This circus provides a more *personalized* experience to our clientele at times. We have a big tent like Samuel does, but here, we allow our audience to step into the ring and investigate the acts for themselves at the start of the show. What you're seeing here is our close-up endeavors."

Grandmother lifts the curtain back that blocks the tent from the outside world and places a hand on my back to shove me forward. I stumble and Elijah loses his grip on my hand.

When I find my footing and look up, I discover a dimly lit tent full of apparatuses and dark, sparkling things hanging from the ceiling. A lyra is suspended in the middle of the tent.

"We want you to perform here, Sienna," Grandmother addresses me. "We don't need Samuel anymore. I want you to design the shows *here*."

"You…want to *leave*?" I couldn't have heard right.

"I've already left. I'm bringing you with me."

"Run—" a voice screams from the side of the tent. It's followed by a loud metal clang. I look over just in time to see a handler slamming a metal rod against the bars of the cage again. A girl cowers on the far side, only inches from where the metal struck.

"What is that—"

"Part of her act," Grandmother cuts me off. "We have unique acts here aside from our main show."

Grandmother waves a hand in the air. Knowing I'm meant to follow, I watch the movement.

"Will you lead?" Grandmother addresses me without looking.

"They want you to be the star act, Sienna," Elijah announces. "They want to feature you. Well, you *and* me."

Nothing makes sense. Why would Grandmother leave Samuel's show? She was training me to take over for her.

The people there are like family. Why would we ever leave for someplace so...*dark?*

Trying not to be too obvious, I carefully move my gaze around the room as I examine it. The slow, deliberate movement gives me a minute to think.

"Grandmother, why?"

"Are you questioning me?" Grandmother whips around to face me.

My grandmother doesn't snap at me. She doesn't even raise her voice to me. She's a master at leveraging disappointment to make people feel a thousand times worse than if she yelled at them.

The magic spell breaks around me. They lied.

Magic isn't real, my inner voice reminds me.

I was foolish to think it might be true. It was ridiculous of me to believe the whispers of the people calling my grandmother magical. I was naïve to believe that a pretty boy who brought me stories of magic might actually be telling me the truth...might actually want to be with me instead of manipulating me.

What if he doesn't know?

"Elijah," I whisper, stepping back.

The man posing as my grandmother drops his façade. He steps toward me dangerously.

"Elijah!" I whisper harshly again, trying to step back to run.

The man I thought was my friend grabs my wrist, clenching down on my bones, refusing to let me leave.

I'm going to pay the price for my wishful thinking.

"Hold her," the tall man growls at Elijah.

Elijah instinctively wraps his other hand around my wrist and I'm certain it will bruise. If these men want me to work for them, they should be more careful of damaging my hands—I need them to climb.

Elijah transforms, no longer pretending to care, leaving me no doubt that the man I thought I was getting to know can't actually be trusted. I drive my heel into Elijah's foot, and he yelps. Thankfully, my dominant hand is free of his grasp, leaving me the ability to strike. I connect with his nose violently. His head reels back—both with the force of my punch and with the shock of the assault— and blood trickles down his upper lip as he glares at me.

"*Stupid* girl."

Pain radiates through my jaw as his knuckles connect.

CHAPTER FIVE

THERE'S ONE SPOT OF BRIGHT LIGHT BEHIND MY EYELIDS. I can tell it's not natural light—it's sharper. It resides only on my left side. It's painful.

I don't open my eyes—I know better. I might not know enough to not trust co-workers who are actually strangers, but at least I know *that* much.

Listening, I pick up the sounds of a circus. *Am I home?*

The more I hear, the more I'm certain I'm not.

Elijah hit me.

No. Elijah *retaliated* when *I* hit *him*.

I'm at their circus—him and that man that was with us.

Grandmother. Where is she?

I had heard her before Elijah and that man talked me into leaving. They must have her too.

I was such a fool.

"Release her at once!" Ida's voice fills the room. She's

here. They have her. I can hear her struggling against them, but they're much stronger than she is or ever has been.

My eyes fly open—I can't help it.

Through my bars, I see Grandmother standing between Elijah and the man, two other men standing near them to provide support. The man who tricked me holds onto Grandmother's upper arm, just above her elbow as she snarls at him.

"What have you done?" She turns, glaring at Elijah. "I gave you a home."

"And he's giving *you* a new one, so even trade," the tall man snarls back. His hair looks greasier than before, but his face is still drawn down into a permanent scowl—I should have seen this coming.

I let a pretty face and cunning words seduce me into letting my guard down. The names I call myself aren't nearly harsh enough.

"She's in a *cage*!"

"Are you volunteering to join her?" The man raises an eyebrow.

Pushing myself upright, I grab hold of the bars. I'm in a giant birdcage, covered in ornate swirls. There's a short, but wide chandelier inside with a hook for what I'm assuming must be a lyra. The bottom is open, leaving the dirt exposed—if they leave me in too long, I'll dig myself out.

Elijah notices me and grins, though it's more like a sneer. He saunters over to me, never taking his eyes off of me. Removing one hand from his pocket, he grasps the bar above my hand.

My nostrils flare as my ears pull back like an animal's might. Every sense is heightened as I watch him.

"Come now, you didn't really think it would be so easy to win a man over, did you? Who do you think I am, your little friends?"

"I'm impressed you can still talk after the way I hit you, Elijah. I figured you'd have at least a few broken teeth with the way you reeled back." There's nothing I can do inside the cage except use my words to lash out at him. He glares.

"You were so willing to believe I'd ever consider caring about you…"

"You were so quick to run your hands down my backside while you kissed me. You didn't seem to mind that." I'm loud enough that the tall man and Grandmother hear me, each making a face. I wish I had Harriet's talent for spitting fire right now so I could singe the fool in front of me.

The tall man's expression changes for a moment—perhaps I've made him wonder who Elijah is loyal too. It's certainly not me, but if I can use it to drive a wedge between them, I'll do it, even at the expense of humiliating myself further.

Looking down, I run a single finger over the bottom of Elijah's hand still resting on the bar above mine. He pulls back in disgust. I smile.

"Luther, you will release my granddaughter," Ida demands.

Luther?

My mind explodes in seven different directions. We've all been warned to stay away from Luther and his unsavory circus. Reports said he was nowhere near us, though. He shouldn't be here.

"He's been following us," I whisper to myself.

"Figured that out, did you?" Elijah whispers back, keeping our conversation private as if it's some sort of game. He pauses as if considering me. "You know, we *could* have some fun while you're here..."

"Dismemberment?" I ask, knowing he doesn't mean kissing.

Elijah scowls at me. "You don't need all of your fingers for your act, do you, Sienna?"

"You take one, I'll take one." I grin back at him, threatening him. He can't risk losing part of his hands—he needs them for his magic act.

"Elijah!" Luther snaps. The boy whips around. "Handle her."

Luther shoves Grandmother toward Elijah. She stumbles for a moment but catches herself. When Elijah reaches her, he pulls her across the tent.

"Sienna!" she screams. I reach through the bars, but since she was never close to me to begin with, it's just an emotional reaction. I call back to her as Elijah drags her away.

I will not cry. I will not cry.

Grandmother is pushed into a cage across the tent similar to my own. I know she can't see me from so far away, but I see her. I'll make it my mission to watch over her from my prison.

Once the men stalk out of the tent, I look around. The girl who tried to warn me is eyeing me from her cage. She's far enough away that we'll have to raise our voices to be heard—we'll have to be careful if we try to talk to keep from being overheard. It's too dangerous to risk now and she raises a finger to her lips with a slight shake of her head.

With nothing else to do, I examine my surroundings. The cage is made of dark metal and made to look worn even though it's kept in relatively good condition. While it looks like part of it is flaking, the entire thing is smooth.

Glancing up, I eye the hook inside the cage. It's high—higher than I can reach. It won't do me any good, unless—

I slip my cloak off. Draping it over one arm, I move to the side of the cage and try to scale the bars. It's not as easy as climbing my silks, but it doesn't take too long until I reach the curved top. Inverting, I hang upside down off the bars, hair dangling behind me.

My wrists and feet wrap around the bars, and I extend one arm, holding the cloak. Upside down, I attempt to hang it on the hook for the lyra. Folded in half, it's long enough for me to reach the ends from the ground, but not long enough to use to wrap. If nothing else, I can use it to swing and propel myself at the men when they open the cage door.

In the air, I realize the knife has been taken from my belt. Shifting my ankle against the bars, I discover that knife missing as well—Elijah must have seen me hide it there. I wonder what other information he's given to Luther over the last two months. Clearly, enough about Grandmother to capture her.

Once I'm sure the cloak is secure, I hold the bars with my hands and dangle my feet. When I'm positioned correctly, I drop to the ground. The girl squints at me from her own cage. For a moment, I almost use hand gestures to point out my plan, but I can't be certain she hasn't been planted here by Luther and Elijah to spy on me. Perhaps it's best not to make friends here.

An hour passes before anything happens, leaving me to study my surroundings outside of the cage. Two men walk in, appearing to be guards. One sets a tray in front of the girl in the other prison. She waits until he's backed up before reaching through the bars to get the food he brought.

A light switches on, plunging the edges of the room into darkness as the light focuses on the lyra hanging from the top of the tent. Black beads glitter all over the ceiling in the form of strings and chandeliers.

The light catches the dust in the air. It sparkles as it floats around the black lyra. It would almost be beautiful if it weren't so terrifying.

A click sounds and the lyra begins to lower.

The men step toward me, pulling their hands out from behind their backs where they had been in resting position. I take a step back, feeling every muscle in my body tighten. Now isn't the time to fight, but I want nothing more.

The one who hadn't approached the other girl unlocks my cage, opening the doors. He motions me forward, lips in a tight line. I breathe out before stepping forward.

They turn, aligning themselves with me as I step out. I walk toward the lyra, assuming they want me to go where they have lowered it to hover above the ground.

"Cooperating. Good." Luther steps out of the shadows. "I'm sure you're aware that your grandmother is just over there."

He points through the shadows to where Grandmother's cage is hidden somewhere in the darkness. I can barely make out things a few feet away with the blinding lights on me, much less determine where they're holding my grandmother.

"You will perform this evening. You will perform *every* evening," Luther informs me. "If you don't, she pays the price."

Grandmother gasps somewhere in the darkness. Elijah chuckles from the same direction. I grit my teeth. If I have the opportunity to destroy Elijah for this, I will.

"How did you get her here?"

"Elijah proved to be a very good source of information for us. He's been spying on you for months. He tried to follow Ida, but lost her. Thankfully you pointed him in the right direction, and while you were distracted with that tiger escape, he was able to get information to us. We reached her before you did."

So, Elijah was the one who released Babur. He let the tiger go then wandered into the woods with me—that was brave of him. Or perhaps he's as clueless as he believes *I* am.

"Clearly not by much."

"We moved her locations, didn't we?"

"And then Elijah brought me right to you," I remind him.

"As he should have. You're going to be more useful to us than your *magical* grandmother will ever be, assuming you prove to be as good as he says you are."

I glower at him.

"All this based off a ridiculous bracelet." He pulls it from his pocket and drops it on the ground, grinding it into the dirt with his heel. "Good thing I pulled it off her while she was trying to escape."

"Good thing Elijah told you how she speaks and acts so you could pretend to be her," I spit back.

"Yes, that was rather helpful." He runs his hand over the edge of his long jacket. "Elijah can clean this up when you're done."

He taps the bracelet with the toe of his shoe before looking back up at me, mouth drawing down into a scowl once more.

"Move," Luther instructs, nodding toward the lyra. "Show me what you're capable of. You'd better live up to expectations, girl."

I close my eyes once I reach the apparatus and take hold of the metal. It feels familiar under my touch. If Luther wants to be impressed, I'll impress him.

I twist, starting to spin the lyra. While still on the ground, a lyra can spin exceptionally fast. Once in the air, it's not nearly as quick, so I keep my feet down and let it carry my body in tight circles. Once I feel I'm moving enough to be impressive, I lift my legs to the lyra. Threading them through, I pull myself up with my arms to sit inside the lyra.

I pull my legs back so my knees hook over the edge of

the apparatus, arms stretched above my head to support myself. Stepping my feet onto the edge of the lyra one at a time, I push myself upright so I'm standing hunched over. Pushing my knees away from myself, I shift my weight directly over my toes to balance myself and push my chest and head outward into a cameo, hands sliding down slightly while I drop my knees just a bit.

Luther comments to Elijah who has joined him, but I can't hear their words from my place on the lyra. Raising my hands higher, I shift to place my head behind the hoop and hook my toes.

Now that I'm closer to the top of the tent after having been raised in the air, I can easily see the chandelier beads—they look cheaply made, but who am I to judge? Instead of dwelling on it, I extend my arms out, leaning back. My legs straighten, pushing the base of the hoop away from my body. I dramatically release one leg and extend it backward in an oversplit before bending it back even further, angling my leg and knee.

"You can do better than that," Elijah calls.

Glaring at him, I lift my leg back to the lyra and walk my legs back onto it until my knees are hooked. Pulling myself up, I continue to walk myself forward until I'm sitting on the hoop in the seated position.

The lights flash, changing color and direction as I move one hand low on the lyra and shift my position to sit sideways so the hoop is resting directly down my spine and seat for balance. Somewhere, music starts to play a creepy melody. I've always enjoyed dramatic mood music, but something about this feels off—perhaps the out-of-tune C sharp messing up the A major chord.

My long leg lifts up to rest inside of the lyra, pushing against it at a right angle at the same time I lay back into the hoop. I rest the muscle alongside of my spine against the lyra and concave my back into it as I position my other leg below the first. My higher leg extends to the top of the lyra and I point my toes up while pressing in with my ankle for balance. I release my hands, using the rest of my body to hold myself in place.

I fall into rhythm with the music, moving along with the tempo as they lower the hoop again. Pulling myself upright, I sit sideways, twisting back into the seated position. Dismounting, I reach back up with an underhand grip far enough apart that both of my ankles can fit between them.

The lyra spins as I lift my feet, hooking them over the edge of the lyra. I flex my toes back down toward myself and release my hands, gracefully straightening my spine until I'm hanging by my ankles as I spin.

If they want a show, I'll give them a show.

I pull myself into an amazon, resting my weight on my neck and shoulder as the rest of my body dangles in the air. Reaching back, I lift one of my legs back with my free arm, nearly touching my head.

Twisting a leg over the lyra, I pull my body up and over until I flip around entirely, circling the hoop several times as it spins. Turning again, I sit on the hoop, leaning back into it to release my hands. I dip my head back to help spin faster, then lift both legs up to the top of the hoop, wrapping one around the tie at the top.

With each turn of the lyra, I maneuver my legs, spinning my body as the men working the rigging raise it up again, following my movements. I flip around a few times until I drop into a Russian split. With one leg high in the air, I arch around until I'm dangling from the lyra upside down, leg still pointed out as the music continues plunking away.

With a quick movement, I drop my legs so one rests in front of the hoop and one rests behind. I sit on the apparatus, straddling it. As soon as I touch it, I release my hands, dropping my upper body below me. Luther gasps beneath me and I try to hide my satisfied grin.

Extending one leg, I rest on the back of one knee from the hoop. I use my hands to pull myself through my leg, contorting myself around it as I spin. The lyra turns as I reach up and pull myself through the hoop, flipping over it until I drop down, dangling by one elbow as the lyra lowers once again.

Once my feet touch the floor, I spin the lyra, releasing it as I bend over backward to look at my captors. They look hungry—like they just found their meal ticket.

The music continues, but I do not. Righting myself, I turn on my heel to face them. Luther no longer looks impressed.

"You've done well, Elijah. Take her backstage and get her ready. She will go on tonight."

Elijah grabs my elbow roughly. I bump into him, hoping to pick his pocket while he's busy paying attention to his master. Maybe he still has my knives on him and I can stab him before threatening Luther until he releases Grandmother.

Jerking my arm away from Elijah to cover my movements, I find only a pack of cards too big to hide on my person. If he had been wearing one of his costumes, I would have known exactly where to look in the secret pockets—I saw Grandmother and Josephine making his wardrobe.

He pushes me across the tent, past my cage where my red cloak is still hanging. He notices it and grumbles a question about why it's there.

"It was too warm to wear it and I didn't want it getting dirty on the ground," I respond.

Outside, the sun glares so brightly that I have to lift a hand to shield my eyes. It leaves a green hue everywhere I look.

"Move," Elijah commands. He doesn't bother to pull the cloth back before shoving me into another tent.

This one is covered in bolts of fabric and trunks. A

young girl looks up from where she's bent over a dark steamer trunk. Her hair is knotted and snarled, making a tangled mess of her white-blonde hair.

"Dress her." Elijah's words are harsh. He clearly went into the right business—he's very good at deceiving people and making them see exactly what he wants them to see. I once thought he had been charming.

The girl scurries over to me, sizing me up.

"What do you do?" she asks quietly.

"Aerialist."

She hovers around me for a moment, grabbing my arm and moving me around. When she's satisfied, she motions me across the room to a trunk. Elijah watches closely from the entrance.

The girl picks through outfits in the truck, handing me things to hold. I fold them over my arm and wait.

When she's done, she directs me to a screen that's clearly thin enough to see my outline through with the light in the background. Elijah doesn't appear to be moving. The girl flips on a light in front of the screen to help compensate.

Behind the thin fabric, I'm ordered to strip off my clothing. I drop it in a pile on a small stool with ripped fabric. The girl has the decency to look away and hands me my new wardrobe. Horrifyingly, Elijah and I would look stunning together in an act if we didn't hate each other. My dark outfit sets off my eyes and hair in the tiny scratched mirror behind the divider.

Elijah doesn't look impressed when I step around from behind the screen, though his eyes spark, telling a different story. He controls his face well.

"Happy?" I ask.

The skin-tight black costume hugs my curves—at least I won't get caught if they have me work with the silks. I miss my vibrant reds—they set my hair off more, and any reminder of Elijah's deceit only serves to infuriate me. Then again, upon further reflection, I suppose I fit more along the lines of Samuel's black and white stripes with red accents than Elijah's all-black outfit. If only they'd let me have a few pops of color like our real ringleader wears.

I wonder if anyone noticed we are missing yet.

"Over here," a new, female voice interrupts. I hadn't noticed the older girl standing off to the side. She must have entered the tent while I was changing.

I take a seat where she motions, Elijah close behind me. He hovers over the girl intimidatingly and she ducks slightly, cowering in his presence. I didn't realize Elijah had such power.

"Just keep them closed," the girl whispers loud enough for Elijah to confirm she isn't conspiring with me. She lifts a brush to my eyes and I lower my lids in compliance.

My fingers wrap around the bottom of the stool's seat, grounding me while I have my eyes closed. Brushes flick over my face, adding powders and creams while the girl paints on my makeup. The girl who gave me my wardrobe, moves behind me, tugging at my long, dark hair. Thankfully, she's careful of my jewelry and doesn't pull at my earlobes.

If it were Fannie and Blanch working on my styling, I would be relaxed and enjoying myself as I was pampered. Instead, my muscles start to burn from being so tight and on edge. Pain creeps into my neck and shoulders where the tension is taking hold. I have to fight against cringing each time the brush comes in contact with my skin and my only thought is whether or not the tools are sanitary.

"It's *fine*," Elijah grumbles as the girls continue to work on my appearance. I don't think I've ever sat in hair and makeup for so long in my life—and it *never* takes this long when I do it myself, which is almost always.

I open my eyes just in time to see the girl with the brushes swipe the soft bristles at my face again, missing as Elijah jerks me away. I stumble across the tent to the door, this time he flings the fabric open as we move exiting at the same time.

The sun is starting to sink into the sky. It's still light out, and will be for a few more hours—well into the show this evening—but it must be late afternoon already. Men stand around talking to each other. They look like they've been doing hard labor all day, clothes and skin covered in dirt. I wonder if any of these men were the ones who brought my hostage grandmother back to this madness after Luther and Elijah tricked me into joining them.

"You're performing tonight. Don't give us any trouble," Elijah instructs, hissing in my ear. "We don't have time for you to come up with a new routine, so you'll just have to figure it out as you go for a few days until we have time to work on this. You *can* base it off of the music, *can't* you?"

He looks at me as if he's actually concerned. I blink, refusing to nod. He knows I can develop a routine as I go —he's watched me do it before. I wonder if his own standing is on the line since he's the one who brought me into this mess. If Grandmother wasn't locked in a cage here, I'd mess up my routine just to hurt Elijah.

"Starting tomorrow, you'll be assisting me in my show as well."

The last thing I want is to be his assistant.

"What does Luther do? Isn't he your magician here?" I realize, wondering why his mentor allows him to take the spotlight off of him.

Elijah turns, glaring at me. "Of course not. He's in charge—he's our ringmaster."

"I thought you apprenticed for him."

The tents flash by us as my captor directs our path.

Instead of going back to the main tent, he wheels us around it. I have to jump over piles of rope as we go. He walks much faster when he's on a mission.

"Luther took me in. I apprenticed once, but it was a lifetime ago. I've been with him for years."

"What is your stake here?" I ask, pulling my elbow away from him so I can walk on my own. "You had a home with us—why give it up for *this*? It seems so oppressive here."

Elijah's steps hesitate for a moment and I move my hands, ready to block him when he tries to throw me against something. He doesn't.

"I have more power here than anywhere else. I'm in charge here."

"I thought Luther was in charge."

"I'm second in command. He trusted me enough to come get you, didn't he?"

"You were really sent on a mission to kidnap *me*?" I ask incredulously.

"I was sent on a mission for Ida. It was easy to gain her trust. When I showed up in the woods with some story about accidentally running into her, it was easy for me to talk my way into staying. I made sure she was in the exact right spot for Luther's men to capture her.

"In case you don't realize, I spent an awful long time trying to keep you away from her out in those woods. It wasn't until I realized you were just as valuable that I allowed you near her."

He turns to grin cruelly at me. The low, dangerous music slithers through the fabric of the tent to us, accentuating his vile reaction.

"You were foolish to believe your grandmother could have actually found magic—there's no such thing, Sienna. There's only reality and deceit. We sell a lie to the people who come to watch us—we make them believe there are good things in this world when it's really just shrewd people that are cunning enough to outwit the commoners ruling over the gullible ones."

"Are you saying you're some kind of king?"

"I'm saying that people are shocked by *your* show—but they truly *believe* mine by the time they leave this tent, Sienna. Give it a few weeks after a show and they'll forget your flashes of red in the sky, but they'll never forget the man who broke their idea of reality. I give them a fantasy that they want to believe in, and then prove to them it's true —and only the best can exist in a world where magic is *real.*"

"It's *not* real," I protest.

"It's as real as the chains you're going to be wearing if you don't cooperate, *Red Girl.*" He stops at an entrance on the far side of the main tent. "Remember—you will do everything I say, or Ida will pay the price."

Directly inside the entrance to my right, is the cage

Grandmother is sitting in. They've given her a small chair, but it can't be good for her hip.

"Grandmother." I announce my presence, knowing she won't recognize me without my signature color on. I grab the bars as she stands.

"Sienna," she whispers. "Are you all right?"

"I'm fine, Grandmother. Are you okay?"

"I'll be fine, dear. Just do what they tell you to do—we don't need you getting hurt." Her fingers, gnarled with age, brush over my hand. "They're keeping you across the tent?"

"Not for long," Elijah interrupts. "We'll be clearing the tent for this show. You'll all be moved. We need the apparatuses."

"Boss said to leave them," a man announces, walking over to us from across the tent. "They perform or they lose a finger."

"The old lady can't perform anymore," Elijah protests. "Besides, who would want to see that?"

"Boss said she works, or she pays." The man shrugs.

"You expect her to flip around on silks all night?"

"Give me a lyra," Grandmother interjects. "I can sit and do some limited moves. At the very least, I can spin and move inside the hoop."

"You can't be serious!" I exclaim. "You haven't done aerial in the last decade."

Grandmother turns to the men proudly. "She's been the star since she was eight."

They both narrow their eyes at her.

"You can't make her work." I look pleadingly at Elijah.

"Looks like you'll be staying here, Ida." He ends the debate. "Sienna is going back to her place as well. Move, Sienna."

"You don't look like yourself, dear." Grandmother turns back to me. "You're hard to recognize with all of that on your face."

She's warning me.

"No one will recognize you," she adds.

Maybe she's waiting for Samuel to find a way to save us. I wasn't smart enough to leave a trail—I thought I was among friends. I'm not sure how long it will take them to find us, but I heard the men say that we're moving on after tomorrow's show now that they have Grandmother in their custody. If they don't locate us in time, it's *my* fault.

"Blood is silent, dear," Grandmother calls. *Another code.*

She used to say that to me when I was practicing on the silks. She'd say it looked like I was entwined in a waterfall of blood as I was twisting high above the ground during training. I would constantly talk my way through it, and she needed to remind me not to ruin the effect by distracting people with my murmured words.

Blood is silent was her reminder to keep my head down and turn out a good performance.

Play the part. Put on a show. Do what you must to keep their attention where you want it. Blood is silent.

I don't fight with Elijah as he guides me back to my cage. If Grandmother believes our friends will find us, I'll believe it too. I'll play along until they arrive to help us escape. If I'm unrecognizable, that might be a problem, though. I'll need my own signal to give them—perhaps my cloak hanging in my cage will help.

"When you're not in the air, you'll be performing here." Elijah opens the door and motions me in.

My cloak is sitting in a pile on the ground, replaced by black silks. *So much for my idea.* I consider picking it up, but it's a miracle they left it there at all, mixed among the shiny fabric pillows tossed inside.

"Consider yourself a bird." Elijah grins. *A caged bird, maybe.* "Inside your nest, you show off, but don't over exert yourself, and *don't* take the focus off of the person in the center of the ring.

"We have other aerial acts. You just happen to be the best of them. You'll go at the end of that segment of the show right before I go on. You'll wow the crowd with your show, then lead the way for me to come on. While I'm performing, you will sit and watch me closely, swinging—you will not detract from my performance, do I make myself clear?"

"Support the other aerialists. Don't show you up. Got it." I tilt my head, giving him my best unimpressed look.

"See that you don't. He wasn't kidding when he said we'd take fingers. It's not like you're a *magician*, Sienna. People come to this show for magic. You're a clown at best."

"A clown that has climbed higher than you have, Elijah. In every sense."

He frowns, placing a hand on one of the bars of the cage door.

"Test me, and I'll work you until you can't go on any longer, Sienna. I'm willing to allow you to be featured in this show in your own right, but people come to see magic and illusion—you're not needed for that. I can push you until you wither, and it wouldn't even matter. And even if we *did* need aerialists, there are more of you here.

"Remember, Luther doesn't need you in the air to survive, Sienna. He needs you in a chair, doing what your grandmother does. You don't need to perform for that, and you don't need all of your body parts for that either. I can take whatever I want from you."

"With Luther's permission," I remind him. I shouldn't push him—I'm supposed to be laying low—but I can't help it. "I'll do as you say, Elijah. I'll cooperate to protect my grandmother, but if you touch her, I'll burn this circus to the ground and you'll never even see it coming.

I'll play the part perfectly and when you think you have me in compliance, I'll destroy you all. If you keep Ida safe, it won't come to that."

"Get ready for the show," Elijah growls, ignoring my words as he steps away.

I turn, kicking pillows out of my way. The men have obviously just dumped them into the cage instead of arranging them around the outside to give me a place to stand.

I bend to fix them when my world suddenly goes black.

Looking up, I see dark fabric draped over my cage, concealing me from the world until it's showtime.

CHAPTER SIX

I PACE AROUND MY CAGE IN THE SEMI-DARK. ONCE MY EYES adjust, I can see my surroundings very dimly, giving me the ability to walk without tripping, but I'm forbidden from touching the fabric until my new handlers remove it.

Elijah hasn't spoken to me since my world went dark, despite me begging him for more information on how this show was going to work. I don't know if there is an opening act or if I'm banished behind the curtain until the aerialists go on. I don't even know *when* they go on in the lineup, leaving me to hover near the silks so I'm ready when I'm exposed to the world.

The music seems to go on forever and I eventually decide that I'm not a part of the opening act. I can't even tell what the opening act is. No one speaks from the center ring. If there's a ringmaster, he's nothing like charismatic Samuel.

I prop the pillows up, trying to display enough of my red cloak to remind me to stay grounded and keep my head down. I don't know what to expect and I don't want to lose my head at the wrong time. The crowd won't know it, but it's a symbol to them too—I'm not of this dark, gothic place. I'm Red.

Once the music shifts, I wonder if it's all been an interlude up until this point and the show is actually *just* beginning. Beyond the curtain, I can hear the crowd so close it's almost like they're right outside of the cage.

When the fabric moves, I jump. I hurriedly pull myself into the silks, ready to perform. The curtain drops around me outside of the cage, revealing men. They gawk at me through the bars, some with their wives. A few couples have children with them, clinging to their legs. These are nothing like the people who come to *our* circus for the shows.

The children look horrified at me while their mothers pale, unable to look away from my face. My makeup must be very strange.

"She looks like she's been hit and died," one boy says.

"It's just pink makeup around her eyes," his father replies, picking him up. "And she's very pale, but never you mind."

They must have used a white powder on me and pink eyeshadow like they did for some of the performers I saw earlier. What a strange choice.

The wife looks down at my outfit with obvious disdain.

More men crowd around to watch me as I swing in the silks, having forgotten to put on a show. Through the bars, I spy another cage—the girl from before—wearing white powder and pink diamonds over her eyes. Her hair is frizzy and voluminous.

I still don't know what they did to my hair, but from what I can tell, it's similarly styled, enough product in it to form an actual bird's nest.

On the other side, another cage is occupied by a man wearing a large cape made of black feathers that reaches partway down his chest and back. He wears a dark, sharply pointed crown on his head with black powder makeup stretching from his hairline down below his eyes to his mid-nose. Black chains cover his arms, and he wears black, short half-trousers as he swings. His lips are outlined in dusty pink that matches the girl's makeup next to me.

The majority of the group standing in front of me moves on to the next cage as more men and women rotate in front of me. In the center of the ring, workers are rolling several cages around the ring through the spectators. They watch closely as a girl in a white corset and skirt twists around a lyra that she obviously doesn't know how to use. Her faux rabbit ears accent her pink lips and she adjusts the ruffled collar she wears, oblivious to the fact that I'm watching her from across the room.

It appears the opening act is designed to let people peer into the cages up close. I hadn't understood what Luther meant this morning, but now I do. The cages shift and wind their way through the crowd, looking at each man and woman behind bars, twisting to the music. Some men linger by the acts that fascinate them, following them if they're in moving cages.

Outside of a cage, several thirty-year-old men dressed all in black with pale makeup and dark eyes circle around the spectators, frightening children, harassing women, and drawing the attention of the men to the girls in the cages. They wear black hats with white accents on them and black folded collars so big that if they sat on a chair, leaned their necks forward, and pulled up their legs, the collars would consume them entirely, hiding everything but their faces. One wanders next to me and reaches in the bars toward me. I know better than to kick him, but I have to fight every instinct to avoid doing it.

The girl in the cage next to me catches my attention, giving me a look to snap me out of my haze. I agreed to perform and I'm not.

Stretching up, I lock myself into the silks and start to move enough to be interesting. I avoid my signature moves or anything complicated that would better serve the show I must give later this evening.

Every time a leering man reaches into the bars to try to brush against me as I move, I shift, avoiding his touch. Unable to see the entire way around myself at all times, many of them manage to touch my legs, lingering against my skin, making me feel sick.

A new cage rolls past me. The girl's hair is braided tightly in buns on either side of her head above her ears. She wears pale powder and has a beauty mark painted high on her cheekbone. Her lips are partially untouched, only a smear of purple is painted down the center of her mouth like tiny lips. Purple, orange and pink crowd her eyelids with no blending, making her face look stark and harsh.

Another hand touches me and I flip over on instinct, avoiding him. When I right myself, another cage spins past me. Elijah is inside—the spinning cages must be for those who cooperate—moving cards from one hand to another as he performs small illusions in an overly pronounced way. His lips are dark, with strange, uneven lines painted out from each side. Hair wild, it stands out as much as the short black tulle collar around his neck.

If this is Elijah's idea of a good costume, why on earth did he pick that gorgeous wardrobe that he wore when he was with us? I wonder if his personal style doesn't fit the aesthetic of his master's show. Or maybe he has more than one style. The gigantic buttons on his white shirt under his sharp suit jacket suggest he might be compensating for something here at this show.

A blonde girl suddenly appears from a lyra high above the crowd at the center of the tent. Her hair is short and curly, topped with a plumb colored feathered hair piece. She holds a cane in her hand. She poses with her high-heeled feet up against the inside of the lyra, lace tights on full display as she opens the show. After a moment, once the crowd looks up to see her, she uses the cane to direct people back to their seats before she continues.

A hand grabs my outer thigh from behind and doesn't let go, cupping his hand around my skin and I panic.

"I'm here, Red," the voice murmurs. He leaves his hand on me, waiting for me to recognize him, then pats my leg twice before slipping away, dragging his hand across my skin.

Ephraim is covered in black as he walks away from me. His fair hair is pulled back into a tight ponytail behind him, barely long enough to hold. He reminds me of Samuel with his hair back like that. When Ephraim turns and sits, his eye is covered in a deep bruise.

He nods before tearing his eyes off of me.

Ephraim is here. He knows where we are and he's here to help us.

I'm surprised Ephraim recognized me the way they have me painted, but maybe my cloak in the bottom of my cage served as more than just a reminder to myself. I glance down at it and see it's been pulled slightly away from the pillows I tucked it between—he's definitely seen it.

My friend glares off to the left from his seat. I follow his gaze for a moment as he watches Elijah's cage spinning in the distance out of the way.

He clearly knows Elijah is in on this and he's trying to keep Elijah from identifying him in the crowd—that's why he's dressed so strangely and has his beautiful locks pulled back into that hideous look. Ephraim scoots over, blocking himself as much as possible with the people sitting in front of him as the cages in the middle of the ring move around, bringing our former coworker closer to him. I can't take my eyes off of him.

A sharp bang on the bars of my cage does the trick as one of Luther's men glare at me. Pulling myself higher in the silks, I move into a cross back straddle, hanging upside down with my legs out to the sides.

The workers clear out the cages from the center of the ring and I realize other acts were also in the moving stages. Elijah gives me a wild look as he's wheeled past me. I pull myself up in response.

Once he's out of eyeline, I turn back to Ephraim. He catches my eye and I immediately lift both legs up into the air, pointing harshly at Grandmother's cage across the tent. He nods sharply once, indicating that he understands.

The bruise on his face takes the most getting used to. I'm terrified of what he had to endure to get to us. Did Luther's men find him? Did he run into Elijah and that's how he discovered us here? Regardless, he's been hit. Ephraim has endured a great deal of injuries over his time with Samuel's circus, but usually his face is protected. I don't even remember the last time someone was able to get the upper hand on my friend.

The girl on the lyra begins her act, only stumbling over a few of the transitions as the people below gasp and call out in response. Under our training, she could go really far with her performance. Here, I imagine, they will work her until she falls to her death and then immediately replace her without a second thought.

I take my time progressing through different moves on the silks. Why waste my energy before my actual performance? The beads glitter from the ceiling, the chandeliers are lower now to give the audience a better view, and I slowly move my legs out while locked in the silks to show I'm making an effort.

After a while, I fall into the rhythm of the music, finding beauty in it where there's meant to be none. Once the lyra is lowered, the girl runs off as the handlers bring a new performer in. They attach silks to the hoop, limiting some of her movements. She doesn't seem as experienced as the first girl so I don't think it matters as much. The girl goes through her act and they lower her back to the ground.

Two more cycle through, both on silks. The second girl—the one who tried to warn me—nearly falls, prompting the audience to gasp as she tangles in the black and white striped fabric.

Luther opens my cage door, motioning me out. He's dressed in dark show clothes. He wears a feathered collar but leaves his stringy hair hanging down in front of him. Sequins sparkle on his jacket, demanding the world watch him.

He holds his hand out to me without smiling—no one smiles here. I take it with my left hand, allowing him to guide me out into the open. I rush to keep up with him as he spins me around in front of the audience. I dip when I feel pressure over my wrist, thrusting my free hand out to the side in a slight bow.

Luther guides me to the silks, bowing to me before running backward. In this show, he is the guide and the whole audience watches in rapt attention for where he leads them. If he tells them I'm the one to watch now, they will.

I catch Ephraim's gaze in the audience, still clearly watching for Elijah so he doesn't give himself away. He nods again, telling me to perform.

The music starts and I climb the silks, blocking out

everything but the off-key music. I invert, wrapping the silks around my body in preparation.

The audience gasps each time I drop, cascading toward the ground only to catch myself at the last second. Luther stands to the side, watching and waiting in case he needs to run in to control me if I step out of line.

Before the music slows, I release my hold on the silks and rush across the tent to where a lyra still hangs low to the ground out of the way. Luther starts to run after me and I smile, knowing I caused him to work when he didn't have to.

I twist onto the lyra, spinning it quickly on the ground before pulling myself up. I catch a flash of Luther halting his run when he realizes I was improvising in the show. He dips into a low bow, directing the audience to applaud me.

I move into an amazon, dangling by my neck and shoulder to much applause. If Luther and Elijah want me to make a name for them, I'll give them a show to remember once I've escaped.

Looping around the lyra, I slip to the ground. Once again, I spin it, this time lifting myself up enough to get my head above the bottom of the hoop. Tipping my neck back, I hang, releasing my arms so I'm spinning on the lyra by only my neck.

I reach back, grabbing my legs to pull them up toward

the back of my head as I spin in the air slowly. The audience erupts as I reach up to steady myself before I pull my body up onto the lyra, swinging my legs until I can walk myself onto the hoop into the seated position.

The men handling the rigging move me up into the air and I sit inside the hoop, moving my legs until I'm perched inside it without using my hands.

When they finally bring the hoop back down, I dismount and rush toward Luther to take my final bow. He grabs my hand, squeezing it tightly enough to know that he's angry I tricked him. I act innocent.

"Get back in your apparatus." His words are threatening. He spins me to bow to the other side.

In my peripheral vision, I see Elijah rushing into the ring.

"I've been told to make this good," I mumble to my captor. He noticed Elijah and nods deftly to me. With a final twirl, he releases me.

I duck under his arm and rush toward Elijah. His eyes grow wider when he notices me, but I don't change my path. My hands collide with his shoulders as I use the force to spin him around. I kiss him on the cheek, surprising him, but the men in the audience shout loudly, making any decent mother in the crowd regret bringing her children to such a show where catcalls are encouraged, and men leer at young girls on stage.

I drag my hand across Elijah's shoulders slowly,

leaving my left arm up in the air as if we were lovers being dragged apart and all I could do was reach for him. After a beat, he raises his arm and pretends to reach for me, even though I'm halfway back to my cage by that time.

Throwing myself in the cage entrance, I leap at my silks, catching myself as I swing. Spinning around the cage, I pretend to keep my gaze on the magician, knowing the audience is still watching me in that moment. Once the silks stop spinning, I quickly step into foot locks and extend into an inverted oversplit, staring at Elijah. When the audience refuses to look away, I release a hand and point, palm up, at Elijah, to ensure they focus on him.

After a moment, I pull myself upright and wrap the silks around my body, finding a comfortable position to hang in, legs extended, body tipped for the audience's benefit, as I swing and stare in Elijah's general direction as he performs. When I'm tired of one position, I move into another, knowing the audience is now mindful of what I'm doing as I keep my attention on the main act. I pretend to watch him dreamily.

If Elijah wants me to keep the focus on him, and has no interest in being with me, I'll make him suffer while I do exactly as he asked me to do.

I risk a look at Ephraim covered by a sweeping gaze

across the audience. He gives me a look before turning back to watch Elijah. Reaching up, he tugs on a strand of his hair. I assume it's some sort of signal, but I don't understand it.

Now that I have nothing to do other than stare, I focus on the intricate design of the edges of the tent. Luther's people have taken the time to black out everything but where they want the audience to focus—the performers.

Unlike Samuel's circus, the environment isn't part of the experience. There are no lights aside from the spotlights used to illuminate the many acts in their cages and the main performer. No ribbons litter the space. The only accents are the beads at the top of the tent and the black cages spread around the room.

Elijah finds his footing after my shocking twist to his performance and works through his illusions, making people disappear before the audiences' eyes, working through a small mentalism act, and creating something out of nothing over and over as the crowd gasps.

Taking a woman's hand from the audience, he guides her down into the ring. He appears just as interested in her as he was in me and I roll my eyes. She giggles as he makes her a part of his act.

I turn, inverting into a cross back straddle again. It's far more entertaining than Elijah and his magical lies.

From upside down, I try to find Ephraim in the audience, but he's not there.

Unable to search for him without giving myself away, I have to force myself to stare at the show. Across the tent, grandmother is in her cage, sitting in the lyra. Thankfully, they gave her a piece of fabric to wrap around her waist, lengthening her skirt. It hangs down in her hand and she twirls it to spin herself in the lyra in the seated position. The chair she had earlier has been removed.

I pull myself up and watch her as she performs. She can't pull her legs up dramatically like I do, but every once in a while, she crosses her legs, or switches to the opposite side of the lyra to add some motion to her time in the hoop. I know she's capable of a bit more, but she's clearly not going to let on that she's capable of more than they think—that will be valuable later.

Grandmother wraps the skirt around her arm, making her look like she has butterfly wings each time she moves to the top of the hoop. I wrap the silks around my arm and mimic her movements gracefully as I rest, tangled in the silks. She can't see me, but it's my silent way of speaking solidarity to her from across the ring.

A movement catches my eye in the audience —Ephraim.

He shuffles to a different seat, moving nearer to the front of the group, inching closer to me. Wisely, he chooses not to look at me, but a few minutes later, he moves again, making his way through the crowd.

Elijah leaves the ring, ushering in a new act. Each one is ostentatious and slightly grotesque. I've never seen a circus so dark, both in color and in feel. Elijah seems to be in his element, as does Luther. Fannie would have a fit if she could see this.

Ephraim looks at me, staring until I turn to look at him instead of watching him from the corner of my eye.

"Trust me?" he mouths.

I nod once, making it look like I dipped my head. I quickly turn in the silks, wrapping them around me to make sure I've covered myself if anyone was watching. I can't let Ephraim get caught—there's enough men here that they could force him into a cage like they did to me, and surely Elijah would make him suffer here; far more so than he will make me pay while under his control.

When I look back to him, he mouths something else. "Tomorrow."

He stands up. I blink. Ephraim makes his way down the remaining steps and walks toward the exit with a scowl on his face as if he's had enough of the show. Without stopping or hesitating, he walks swiftly toward the exit, collar high on his neck to cover part of the short ponytail he's wearing.

I want to call out to him, to beg him to stay, but instead, I twist, dropping in the silks enough to get attention. I don't bother looking; I know he's already gone and walking away from the dark circus tent into the twilight evening.

Tomorrow. He promised me he would be back tomorrow. I just have to survive the night.

CHAPTER SEVEN

SLEEPING ON THE GROUND IS THE LAST THING I WANT TO do, but they don't give me a choice. Once they cover my cage over to prevent me from talking to the others, I tie the ends of the silks together, one higher than the other, to form a hammock they didn't expect me to build for myself. Settling back into it, I cover myself with my cloak even though it's warm out—it's a form of armor for me, protecting me from the world.

Poor grandmother was given a cot, thankfully, but it's anything but luxurious. Even Hoyt's cot near his tigers looks more comfortable and I've sat on it before—it's like sitting on a plank.

Sleep eludes me, but eventually, I sink into a bit of rest. I'll need it for whatever Ephraim is preparing. I worry about how Ephraim got that black eye for an hour before my mind shifts to the escape, and eventually, I find myself lost in sleep.

When I wake up, the fabric surrounding my cage is still there, but bright enough to let me know it's morning. I don't want the men taking away my silks, so I force myself up and untie them before kicking some of the pillows around on the ground—at least they had the consideration to leave those for me. Or maybe they are just lazy.

Blood is silent, Grandmother's words ring in my mind. I will be silent and these men holding us captive won't realize we're escaping until it's too late to stop us.

Before I can sit, the curtain around my cage is ripped away. Luther stands before me. He turns and nods to the man standing beside him. The man opens the door and steps back.

"You did well last night. You might find it easier here than you thought, assuming you don't try to mess with me again." Luther raises one eyebrow at me. "Go get cleaned up and then we'll talk about your future here."

He's awfully willing to work with me knowing I'm likely to escape the first chance I get. I wonder if this is how he controls the others too—holding a family member to leverage against them, forcing them into submission. I wouldn't be nearly so compliant if Grandmother wasn't at risk.

The man with Luther grabs my arm, but I elbow him. "I'm perfectly capable of walking, thank you."

He escorts me to a small tent to wash up and use the

bathroom. A scared girl scurries away as we approach. Inside, I dip my hands under the water and brush it through my hair.

I take a breath and dip my head under the water. It's warm enough that my hair will dry, and I hate going with an unwashed mane. Pulling the water up my arms, I brush it over my shoulders. Not caring if I'm taking too long, I wipe water over my legs, attempting to clean off the dirt. The man yells to hurry up, but I dismiss him, claiming I can't be covered in dirt for the show later.

Wringing my hair out, I let it drip before tossing it over my shoulders. When it air dries, it will become curly and soft, though I'll have to work to brush it out after the tangles they added to it last night. Picking up a towel, I scrub the makeup off my face. I hope it won't be painted back on until after Ephraim finds me.

He must have been alone last night if the others were nowhere in sight. They would have made sure I had seen them if they had been there. They likely would have broken us out during the evening's performance if they had had the numbers.

The man eyes me when I exit the tent dripping wet. My hair is plastered against my back, dripping down in cold streams of water despite being wrung out—long hair holds in water much longer than shorter hair and has a tendency to release it like tiny waterfalls at the worst times.

A few drops hit my ankles as I walk alongside the man. He returns me to my cage, but before he can lock me in, Elijah appears. I sigh and follow him.

Like our own circus, this one has a tent for food. Elijah hovers over me as I sit. He takes the seat across from me and a short man with a wrinkled face waddles over quickly on unsteady feet with two plates. Elijah's is covered in food. Mine has decidedly less.

Picking up a fork, I poke at what some might describe as a food. Elijah doesn't seem to notice and eats his meal.

"That was quick thinking last night," he acknowledges me. "I don't like being surprised, though, so we're going to have to work on it."

He doesn't like being surprised, but he *does* like when I make him look good. Star-crossed lovers being pulled apart by separate acts is certainly good for conversation in the audience and he knows it.

Luther enters the tent and saunters over. He reminds me a bit of Hoyt with the way he walks, but their personalities aren't the same at all—Luther is far too sullen—though they both have huge egos.

"I want you to plan our acts," he addresses me.

"I noticed they fell pretty flat," I murmur, picking up a piece of what I think is egg with my fork. I take a bite. Definitely egg, but not very good. "Have you fed Ida yet?"

Luther ignores me. "We obviously have different acts than you're used to, and quite a few aerialists. You'll need to take that into consideration when you and your grandmother are planning the new show."

At least he plans on letting me see her.

"The makeup needs to go," I say flatly.

"The makeup and wardrobe stay," Luther corrects me as the short man sets food in front of him. Luther eats without looking at me as the older man waddles away. I'm terrified he might fall and break something, like the ankle that clearly never set right the *last* time he broke it.

"Why do you keep people in cages?"

"The apparatuses are for the show," Luther replies, shoving another bite of food into his mouth. I wrinkle my nose—men are disgusting at times. Maybe Ephraim and Orville are extra considerate around us and I've become spoiled.

"I slept in one last night," I point out, setting my fork down. I'm slightly surprised they gave me something I could stab them with.

"That's only for people we can't trust." Luther looks up. "Elijah doesn't sleep in the bird cages."

"Everyone else does."

"Look around, Sienna," Elijah cuts in. "How many people do you see roaming around?"

"You mean the men who threatened the people in cages?" I lock eyes with him. I definitely want to put the fork through the back of his hand.

"I mean the handlers and performers. Work with us,

Sienna, and you might even be able to share our quarters with us." He glances at Luther who nods.

"We're willing to give you some freedoms if you work with us," he concedes. "Just don't cross us and you can earn our trust. Like I said, you could learn to like it here. I saw the way you fell into your performance—you could do well with our type of circus."

"How long have you been here?" I cut him off.

"Two performance engagement. We were only here to find you, Sienna. We don't need to stay, nor do we need to impress these lowlifes. They don't have money to pay for extras and there's no point in wasting our time.

"In fact, we don't even need to stay this afternoon. We could move on to our next stop and it wouldn't hurt our purse one bit."

"We're just doing it to rub it in Samuel's face. When he finds out you're *with* us and performed in the next town over, he'll be livid."

Luther's lips quirk up on one side. "There's nothing he'll be able to do about it. He won't be able to track us, and by the time he finally finds us, you won't want to go back."

This guy is delusional.

He turns his wolfish grin on me. "I'm willing to give you the world, Sienna, if you'll join us. You can run this place. You can be the star act. Your grandmother can help you as long as she's alive. Turn this circus into the most successful one in the country, and I'll give you everything. You'll only have to answer to me."

He'll swallow me whole and spit me out, he means.

"Why are you so willing to give me *everything*?" I ask skeptically.

"He needs to keep this circus open. We've put far too much into this to fail," Elijah answers for his boss.

"So, you're failing?" I respond, picking up my fork again. "Kidnapping all those people isn't getting you anywhere?"

"If you don't want me coercing people to work for me, give me enough star acts that make other performers come to *us* for jobs. I won't need to force people into working if the talent is coming to me."

He makes a good point.

A horse whinnies outside the tent somewhere. A man yells at him as the horse apparently balks. I tune it out and focus on Luther.

"How are you getting all of these people to cooperate, Luther?"

"Same reason you're complying, little girl." He and Elijah share a conspiratorial grin, confirming my suspicion.

"Fine. If I'm going to do this, I still get to use red."

"Excuse me?" Luther drops his smile.

"You heard me. Red silks this evening or I don't go on. If I'm the star, then I'm the star. He gets his weird sparkly suit"—I wave my hand at Elijah—"and I get my silks. There's no room for discussion on this."

"I—"

"Give me my silks and I'll train that little bird in the cage next to me. She almost killed herself last night. I'll even wear that stupid outfit you picked out for me."

Luther starts to object but quickly realizes the merits in my argument and nods. "Fine. You'll have your silks. You'll work with Candace once you're done eating. If I don't see dramatic improvement by this evening, *well…*"

He brushes his hair back as he trails off. Standing, he walks away.

"The show is this afternoon, by the way. You've got five hours. We're moving tonight." He yells over his shoulder like I don't already know that information.

Elijah catches my eye. "I always knew you were reasonable."

"Get my silks, Elijah."

He looks like I slapped him.

"Oh, Elijah." I laugh at him. "Really. Did you honestly think that you'd be above me? I'm saving Luther's circus. I'm training his people. You're doing what—an act? Your moment of glory was bringing me to Luther to work for him. You had your moment, Elijah. This circus is now what *I* say it will be.

"I'm going to train those people in those cages. I'm going to make them greater than you. I'll train them all to do exactly what I do. I'll turn this into a circus of the best aerialists in the country. No one will rival us. By the time I'm done, we won't even need a magician. I'll make the aerialists magical enough for the audience.

"You just took away your own job, my friend. With one *kiss*, you sealed your own fate. You've destroyed yourself with your ambition. You work for me now."

He reels back as I remind him of our searing kiss in the woods yesterday.

"Now." I bat my eyelashes. "If you want my mercy, go get my silks, *boy.*"

Elijah snorts, furious.

I stand up and sway away from the table, leaving the plate and the steaming man behind. He shouts at me, but the men don't dare touch me as I march to the main tent, leaving them scrambling to keep up with me.

Throwing the curtain open, I step in.

"Open the doors," I command loudly, confusing the workers. "Do it."

The man behind me nods as I turn sharply toward him. He heard Luther give me power and knows better than to test me.

I stomp over to the cage next to mine. "Unlock her."

The girl looks at me, terrified.

"I told Luther I'd train you so that you don't kill yourself tonight. I get red silks in return."

She looks terrified at me that I would give in so

quickly. She has no idea that it's all an act until Ephraim launches his rescue mission.

"To the lyra, Candace. We have work to do."

She quickly scurries across the tent to the hoop. I motion for the men to lower it and set to work teaching her basic safety for the moves she had attempted and failed to do last evening.

Five hours pass quickly as I instruct her, avoiding all personal conversation and hoping she catches on.

Ephraim is radiant in red. Whoever decided he should exclusively live in those gorgeous blue costumes was a fool, though, to be fair, he's more striking in his signature color than mine. He still looks incredible sitting in the audience, watching me.

The black eye is gone, leaving me to realize that it was makeup he wore yesterday—Josephine taught him well. He's wearing fake facial hair to hide his strong jawline, but I could identify him anywhere. His eyes spark from across the room as he locks eyes with me.

The entire group is here, spread around the room in disguises. Orville's easy features and soft eyes are trained on me from several rows away from his cousin, also dressed in a variation of red. Hoyt looks as angry as

Babur when he isn't fed on time, hunched forward in the front row on the far side of the room.

Blanch sits near Clarence in the back—I nearly didn't recognize her in that wig—and Fannie and Harriet hover near the door, hair wrapped up in scarves to avoid detection. Out of the hundred people who work for Samuel, half of them are in the audience, and I imagine the other half is waiting outside to help us escape without detection. Samuel is nowhere in sight, though I didn't expect him to show up in a situation where Luther could easily spot him. The two have known each other for many years.

The only one we have to worry about is Elijah—no one else here knows our faces. My friends perceptively watch the show, keeping an eye on me, Grandmother, and the men holding us captive.

Candace does much better this afternoon. I watch from my perch in my cage, wrapped in my silks.

My outfit this evening is different than before. Lace covers my legs under my solid black outfit. Elijah walked into the wardrobe tent and demanded I wear the most uncomfortable outfit possible and I let him have the victory. If he thinks he gained a bit of the upper hand, he's less likely to watch me this afternoon.

When it's my turn, Luther escorts me from my cage and I dance my way over to the center of the ring. My silks drop from the top of the tent, cascading down in red.

Blood. My people are out for it this afternoon.

Hoyt and Ephraim lean forward onto their knees as they watch me. Orville leans back, glancing sideways. I don't know their plan, but I have to be ready for it. I need to get Grandmother and help as many of the caged people as possible before I flee.

"Boo!" someone yells from the audience. It's low and hard to pick out at first, but a second quickly follows.

"We're tired of this!" a female calls—I think it's Fannie using a strange voice.

"It's the same thing over and over!" Orville yells. The crowd picks up their chant and demands something new.

Luther's face crumbles as he realizes his plan is falling apart.

"Do something," he hisses at me as if I would have an answer to saving his precious circus.

"What do you want me to do?" I hiss back as he tightens his grip around my hand, making me feel like he's going to shatter bone if he presses any harder.

"Give them a show!"

"I'm an aerialist—my act is exactly what they *don't* want to see!"

Behind Luther, I can see Blanch and Clarence in the background. She waves at me, trying to get my attention. I ignore Luther, waiting for some kind of signal from my friend. They started this riot—they must have a way to end it.

"Pick Ephraim," Blanch mouths, pointing in his direction. I squint as she repeats her actions.

"I have an idea," I say, pulling away from Luther.

I prance a few feet away, closer to the audience. Raising one hand, I ask them to silence. It takes a moment, but they eventually calm down.

"So, you want something new?" I begin. "If you think this is so easy, why don't you come up here and try it?"

"We didn't come here to do the show ourselves, lady," a man objects.

"What if I could teach one of you to go up there with me? What if I let one of you up close and personal while I'm in the air?"

Several people object, but Ephraim in disguise stands to his feet.

"I'll do it." He leers overtly at me. His eyes drag from my feet up to my face, lingering. He grins at me suggestively—not a side of Ephraim I'm familiar with.

I look him over as if disgusted by his obvious attention toward me. Holding a hand out, I wait for him to begin walking out of the stands toward me. Once it's obvious that he's joining me in the ring, I run toward the silks, bypassing Luther.

"Leave," I murmur.

The silks sway as I launch myself onto them, intentionally spinning. I hold myself between them, moving my feet as if dancing to the music that isn't playing.

When Ephraim gets close, he quickens his steps, and I fling one side of the silks toward him, lowering myself just enough to run on the ground. With one side of the silks in my hands and the other in Ephraim's, we run opposite each other. He moves slower than me as if trying to catch on. Balancing on one arm, I lift the other, signaling the men working the rigging to raise us into the air, holding my hand flat when we're a few feet off the ground to make the audience assume I'm teaching him.

"You okay?" I call to him.

"Keep going, Red," he calls back, smiling. "Teach me your ways."

Pointing down, I signal the men to lower us back to the ground and we both run once our feet touch the ground. Letting go, I spin, twirling the fabric around me until I run to Ephraim.

We hover together as I pretend to give directions for the benefit of the audience. Ephraim leans closer to me, hovering over me while holding some of his weight on his half of the silks.

"Are you going to tell me what's happening here?"

"We're performing, of course," Ephraim says. "I've always wanted to do a duo show with you."

"*You* wanted to do an aerial show with me?"

"You can't teach a man to work on silks and not

expect him to want to show it off with a pretty girl every once in a while." He winks suggestively at me—again, for the benefit of the audience...*right*? "I've got seven different knives hidden on me, by the way. I have a feeling we'll need those later.

I point at his feet and he slips out of his boots. "They're not in there," he informs me. "At the end of the act, be sure to hide at least one on you."

"And where do you propose I do that?" I point as if I'm explaining where I want him to stand. Bending, I demonstrate a foot lock.

"Good point. Let me handle that," he comments. "Just play along."

"Fine." I back up as he does what I just pretended to teach him how to do.

"Come on, already!" an annoying man calls from the crowd. My head snaps in his direction, then I wrap the silks around my wrist and walk quickly in an arc until I lift my feet and spin in a small circle with one hand out, upright to the audience to indicate that I would comply. I point to Ephraim.

"Ready?"

"We'll talk up in the air."

He drops his fabric, letting it float to me. The music starts and I gather the silks in my hands, climbing up into the air. Once I'm high enough, I wrap my feet into a double foot lock and invert into a cross back straddle, gathering the flowing fabric into my hands. Looping each side so it dangles loosely between the ends of my feet and my hands. Grasping it tightly and locking in my wrists, I nod for Ephraim to climb up the silks I'm holding for him.

Ephraim signals the men working the rigging to lower the silks, but I'm only confused for a moment. I nod, giving them permission. They drop the rigging lower and Ephraim saunters over to me, grabbing the silks just under my hand. He points up, nodding to the men working the rigging, and then pulls back, stretching the silks as far as they will go to prepare to swing us.

He pauses before pushing forward. As soon as we move, he lifts his feet off the ground and the men pull us up, sending us toward the top of the tent. We move back and forth once before Ephraim drops, clutching the ends of the silks. He inverts in the air as I hold him. His feet make a running motion as the rigging men bring us back down—at least they're capable of following along with what we're doing in our act.

Ephraim releases his hold, freeing me to right myself. I quickly unlock my feet and wrap myself, twisting in the air for a double star drop. It takes me a moment, but Ephraim keeps the attention on me, reaching out for one side of the silks as it brushes past him.

I drop, leaving the audience in shock.

Twisting in the air, I cascade down toward Ephraim.

He stands there smiling at me. I can barely see him as I twirl in the air, but somehow I feel like I've seen everything. Just as it looks like I'm going to crash into his arms, I jerk to a stop, still wrapped in the silks and he pulls away to let the audience see I saved myself.

"Not bad," he jokes.

I release myself and dance over to him, letting him spin me on the ground. His touch is warm and familiar.

Why haven't we done this before?

"My turn?" he asks. Before I can respond, he rushes to the silks and climbs up. Inverting like I had, he waits for me to join him in the air. I oblige, climbing.

He holds a hand out to me, and I take it, preparing to use him like an apparatus. We go through a series of moves where I contort in the air, held by only a foot and wrist, a single foot, or both feet.

Miraculously, Ephraim talks me through each transition, telling me when he's going to let go or move me. I follow his cues, bending my body as he directs. I didn't know he was capable of holding me like this, but he knows my act well enough to know what I'm capable of doing and he knows his own strength, making him the perfect person to direct our performance.

"Hands," he murmurs, and I turn to let him hold me by my wrists. Pulling my legs between our arms, I twist up around his waist. I lock my legs around him and we both let go, holding our arms to the side. I barely notice the audience cheering.

Looking up, I meet Ephraim's eyes. "We're going to get you out of here, Sienna. I promise."

The lights flash in my eyes, making a glowing ring appear around him, washing out his features. The fake scar stretching across his temple is barely visible.

I take his wrists, pulling my legs from around him. With my knees near my face, holding on only by my wrists, I wait.

"Trust me," Ephraim whispers, letting go of me. I drop.

He catches my ankles, stopping my decent. I twist in the air, facing the opposite direction and kick my feet up until I'm wrapped around Ephraim again. My back rests against his chest as we hang upside down. He pushes me up so that I'm upright. Reaching up, I take hold of the silks and pull myself up, standing on his outstretched arms.

Luther's eyes are wide below us as I glance down. There's no way he believes I *just* taught Ephraim how to do this. "He's onto us," I murmur as I lift myself up to stand on the inside of Ephraim's legs—it's a good thing the man is indestructible.

We quickly do a few moves before I drop back onto his hands, sliding down his arms. I contort in the air.

"When we hit the ground, get ready to go—this was a

distraction to break Ida out." The silks start to lower us slowly, knowing they can't risk Ephraim dropping me if they move too quickly.

"The others?"

"We couldn't trust them, but we won't leave without them. Turns out, Josephine is pretty sneaky—I saw her near Ida for a second while we were working."

"Who is helping her?" I reach up and take his wrist as he flips me in the air. I kick my leg back, posing for the audience.

"Hoyt and Harriet. Fannie is covering them. The rest are here for us. Samuel is waiting outside."

I *knew* our people would be outside too.

"I'm going to beat Elijah to a pulp before we leave," Ephraim comments. "Just warning you now."

"As long as you let me get a kick in, I'm fine with that." I twist the silks in the air to spin us as he holds me in place by my feet.

"Confession: I followed you yesterday. Please don't be mad."

"Ordinarily I would be mad at you for not trusting me, but if you hadn't, I'd be on my way to...*wherever* Luther was planning on dragging us."

I drop the silks and Ephraim switches his hold, taking one ankle and one wrist in his hands. Turning, I look up at him.

"It's not that I didn't trust you." He tries to convince

me. "I didn't trust *Elijah*. I saw him follow you and I followed him."

That means he saw us kiss. Embarrassment washes over me.

"He never should have done that to you," he says softly. "You deserve so much better than that."

Ephraim pauses for a moment, glancing down as we draw nearer to the ground. "Time's up, Sienna. Let's do this."

He holds me in the air until I wrap myself around his waist one more time. I flip forward, taking him with me so he's parallel to the ground, facing the top of the tent. I dangle off of his back as he slides us down the silks.

Once on the ground, the music continues to play, but Luther and his men converge on us.

Suddenly, Ephraim pulls me toward him, slamming me into his chest. He buries his hands in my knotted hair, twisted from how they designed my hair for the evening.

Ephraim's lips are searing against mine, kissing me over and over as he roams his fingers through my hair. I don't intentionally place my hands on his sides and run them up his back, making him shiver. He *definitely* means to make my knees go weak.

When he pulls back, I realize why he risked kissing me as the men converge on us—he's hidden one of his knives in my intricately designed hair. I can fight back.

The audience bursts into applause, cheering for us,

thinking it's all part of the act. Ephraim quickly pulls on his shoes.

"What is this?" Luther demands. "You'll pay for this."

"Ephraim?" Elijah sounds shocked, dark features pulling back tightly. Ephraim rips off the fake facial hair he had been wearing—I'm excited to try kissing him without it.

Ephraim and I separate, pulling away from each other as we run in opposite directions. The silks guide us, pulling us back into the path of the men trying to take custody of us, knives and ropes in hand.

We have one chance at escape, and if we fail, it's going to be a bloodbath.

CHAPTER EIGHT

Ephraim holds onto the red silk as he runs at my captors. Lifting his feet, he slams into Luther, knocking him to the ground. While I move, I wrap the silk around my waist, allowing my hands to be free to fight. The downside is that I'm tangled in a silk, which will make it hard to escape if I need to.

Lowering my center of gravity, I run at Elijah. I know Ephraim will have his say with our former friend and this might be my only chance. I grab hold of the silk with one hand and mimic Ephraim's move, kicking with both feet in the air.

Elijah sees me coming and tries to move out of the way. I collide with him, but he's prepared and grabs one of my arms, spinning me in a tight circle close to his body. He growls angrily at me, trying to slash at me with his fingernails.

I let go of the silk, letting it hold my weight in my

lock. With both hands free, I attack, clawing at his face. The spinning motion continues, forcing Elijah to stumble over his own feet. I cry out as I attempt to take his eye—Grandmother always taught me to go for the eyes if I were ever being attacked, and surely this counts.

Elijah pulls back, giving me the briefest of moments to unwrap myself from my lock. Now is the time to run, not the time to fight tangled in silks.

Ephraim battles against Luther and his men as Orville and the majority of our men join us in the ring. The crowd's shocked gasps chorus around us.

Elijah punches me, snapping my head to the side long enough to see mothers scooping up their children, trying to escape the fight. I don't blame them for fleeing.

Turning back, I take my rage out on Elijah.

"Sienna!" Ephraim warns me. I look over in time to see Luther crawling toward me, ready to pounce.

I realize the music has stopped. It's a strange thing to discover as a man is running at me, but my brain focuses in on how silent it is aside from the people yelling around us and the sound of bodies colliding in battle.

"You belong to *me!*" Luther's words pierce through the chaos around us.

People scream from their cages, begging to be let out. They recognize that this is their chance. Someone else will have to save them.

Elijah reels back, but I don't have time to see what he's

doing. Luther barrels toward me. I drop to the ground at the last second, forcing him to trip over my body on the dirt. Spinning, I kick out, connecting with his chin as he whips around to face me.

He curses at me, grabbing my ankle to jerk me toward him, dragging me through the dirt. Something catches in my sight and I duck instinctively as Elijah sails over my head, missing his target—the fool is trying my move on the silks.

Reaching into my hair, I pull out the knife. Drawing my arm back, I drive the hilt of the knife into Luther's cheekbone. I kick, forcing him to release his grip on me. Scrambling back, Ephraim grabs my wrist, pulling me to my feet.

"I will destroy him." Ephraim's growl is punctuated, looking for Elijah as he swings in the air.

"And I'll let you," I reply.

"Heads up, you two," Orville yells as he rushes past us. "No time for kissing!"

My face drains of color; I can feel it running out of my skin. Ephraim's hand on my hip doesn't help.

He spins us. Our people wrestle with Luther's men. Thankfully, most of them have resorted to hand-to-hand combat instead of using weapons against each other. Samuel's men have the advantage though—he's made sure even our handlers are trained. Luther appears to have only used his men for muscle around his circus and they falter when our men contort easily around their punches.

"You!" Luther bellows. Turning, I follow his gaze. Standing in the light pouring in from the open tent door, Samuel rides toward us on Caleo's back. She picks her trunk up when she spots Orville fighting.

A man snaps Orville's head back, dropping him to the ground. He quickly raises his hand and forces Caleo to stay in place. She obeys, waiting for Samuel to give her directions.

"You thought you could steal my acts?" Samuel yells from atop the elephant. He moves, echoing the commands we're familiar with Orville giving his charges. Caleo responds, stepping forward.

"Where did he go?" Ephraim whispers, pulling my attention away from the leaders of the two circuses.

"Who?" I ask, realizing my arm is wrapped around Ephraim's back, hand sitting on his hip. He turns, moving me with him.

"Elijah. Where is he?"

"I didn't see."

"We need to find him."

One of the chandeliers falls from the top of the tent, crashing next to us. The men working the riggings are trying to assist their boss by dropping things on Samuel's team. It shatters, sending black, metallic beads flying everywhere.

"Careful," I caution Ephraim.

He pulls a knife out from his boot—he must have slipped one in after he returned his shoes to his feet after our act. I, unfortunately, am still without shoes, leaving me to move around the ring barefoot.

"Give up, Luther. You're not going to take my people from me," Samuel calls down.

"Your girl isn't coming back to you, *Samuel*. She knows she can do more with me." Luther leaps to his feet, striding toward the elephant and our ringleader.

I wonder how easy it was to convince Elijah to betray people for fame. It's the only reason I can think of for Luther to assume I would be so easily swayed for power.

"I'm not staying with *you*," I call, still searching for Elijah. I can't find him anywhere.

"Sienna!" Samuel calls, stretching out his hand for me to join him, declaring my allegiance. Four men stand between us, making it nearly impossible. I'd rather fight for my freedom anyway.

"You won't take her or the old lady from me!"

"Ida is already halfway back to our camp, Luther. You lost her during Sienna's performance."

Luther whips around, looking for Grandmother's cage. It's empty, door open. He whips around, ready to attack.

Ephraim raises his left hand, balancing himself as he

retracts his right hand, knife pointed up to the top of the tent as he prepares to throw it at Luther.

"Stop!" Ephraim warns him. He doesn't and Ephraim releases the knife, burying it in Luther's shoulder.

The tall man turns, wild-eyed.

"Knife!" Ephraim directs. I quickly drop my weapon into the knife thrower's hand, and he sinks it into the front of Luther's opposite shoulder. He staggers back, screaming in pain with two knives protruding from his upper arms. He throws curses at Ephraim and Samuel as if they matter.

Then he turns his sights on me.

Ephraim's muscles tighten next to me, brushing against my arm, but he doesn't sweep me behind his back as I expect him to do. Instead, he bends, retrieving another knife from a hidden pocket in his pant leg, and places it in my hand. He nods without looking at me.

I'm not going to kill Luther!

"Leg," he murmurs, as if reading my thoughts.

In the same way that Ephraim has tried the silks with me under our own tent, he's also taught me knife throwing. I'm nowhere near as skilled as he is, but the alternative was learning to be punched in the gut by a strong man, and I wasn't about to go through that training.

Arm in the air, I ready myself as Luther takes slow, heavy steps toward me, wrapped in pain.

"Stop, Luther," I threaten. I give him a few more chances to come to his senses. "I said stop."

When he doesn't, I embed the knife in his leg, forcing him to the ground. He pulls the knife out of his leg and tries to throw it at us, but by that time, Samuel is off of Caleo's back and walking up behind Luther. He pries the knife out of his hand.

"There!" Ephraim shouts. I jump next to him.

Ephraim takes off running, leaving me behind. I rush to keep up with him.

"Guess he's not so loyal now, is he?" I shout to Luther, swinging my arms at my side as I try to keep up with my friend. Luther's face crumbles, enraged as I shoot past him.

"Orville!" Ephraim calls, arms pumping in the air as he runs, the muscles in his back tight.

His cousin had somehow managed to work his way just outside of the tent as he grapples with one of Luther's men—the one that had been my guide this morning.

Ahead, I see what Ephraim saw: a red cape—*my* red cape.

The person turns around, looking over their shoulder as they run, hood high around their face to block people from seeing who it is. Several of our people dart out of the way, assuming the red flash is me. They let the person pass, running straight toward Brisheet.

Orville turns just in time to see Elijah leap onto Brisheet's saddle. He orders his elephant to stay still as Elijah attempts to force her to run. My cape settles around his legs as he kicks the poor elephant.

In the background, some of Luther's now-former captives are releasing the animals. I wished we could have talked to them before the escape to make sure they didn't just let the animals wander off to be hurt or killed by the townspeople. We'll have to collect them when this is all over and get them to new homes. Thankfully, Luther's circus consists mainly of people and not animals.

Ephraim runs to head off Brisheet while Orville shouts to her, trying to calm the poor creature. I run straight for Brisheet and her rider. Launching myself in the air while Elijah is distracted by Ephraim's approach, I pull myself up next to him.

I'm only sitting behind him for a moment before the magician reaches around his back—and mine—and pulls me forward roughly. I land in his lap, sideways. Looking up, I meet his glare.

"Fine, you want to play this way, we will." He pulls out a knife and holds it to my throat. "Back off, Ephraim. I'll do it, and you know I won't hesitate."

Ephraim's hand shoots out to the side, holding off Orville.

"Let her go, Elijah, and we'll let you leave."

It's sweet how Ephraim thinks Elijah will ever consider that as an option.

"No." Elijah laughs. "You won't touch me while I have the flying princess here. She stays with me.

"Besides," he adds, "I'm pretty sure I took her from you once anyway."

Not one of my finer choices. I let Fannie get in my head sometimes when it comes to boys. From now on, I'll ignore them completely.

Unless Ephraim wants to kiss again.

Hoyt runs up, nearly crashing into Ephraim. His eyes dart between Ephraim and me, trying to find some meaning in the scene as his jaw tips open slightly. For a man comfortable working with cranky tigers, he looks a bit bewildered now.

"Elijah, let her go!" Hoyt demands, glaring at the man who has me pinned on top of an elephant.

I try to right myself so I can see them from more than the corner of my eye, but Elijah holds me down, using his forearm to block my upper arm from moving. Unable to twist around, I wait, biding my time.

While Elijah's eyes are on the boys, I stretch a hand down Brisheet's side. Candace's eyes peer out from behind a barrel a few yards away. She holds her breath as she watches the scene. The girl looks like a scared rabbit about to bolt. I shake my head no and she sinks back.

"Trying to be a tiger, I see..." Elijah comments flippantly, still trying to get Brisheet to follow orders. She balks, stepping backward. He's clearly never worked with animals before.

The boys' protests chorus each other to distract my captor as Orville tries to sneak up to Brisheet without Elijah noticing. Unfortunately, he *does* notice, which is when I jerk forward, grabbing the end of the cape he's wearing.

Pulling hard, I force him back, causing him to lose his balance. Elijah grabs onto my waist, trying to steady himself. Instead, I inch my foot up along Brisheet's shoulder and push us over, toppling Elijah backward, while I plummet face first to the ground.

He slams into the ground, and it audibly knocks the breath out of him. I roll, using my hands to propel myself over and I tuck my head as I move, using my feet to catch myself.

I make it upright before Elijah grabs my ankles and forces me back to the ground in a heap. Brisheet rushes away from us heavily and Orville takes off after her.

Ephraim and Hoyt run up to us, but Elijah has found his knife again and is yelling threats. To the right, smoke drifts up into the late afternoon air, dark and twisted. A pile of hay meant for the animals is on fire. Harriet hovers a few feet away, watching the scene unfold, her tools in her hand, ready to assist with her fiery ways. She surprisingly doesn't look nervous.

Blanch appears next to her, cradling a bleeding arm with her hand.

Elijah stands, towering over me, leaving me on my back on the ground. He points his knife at me. Ephraim and Hoyt slow their approach, trying to keep him from doing anything rash.

Threatening the wolf will do me no good—that doesn't throw him. If I want to distract him and give my people the upper hand, I have to do something to fluster him.

Raising my right foot, I drag it along his ankle, under his pant leg. My nose wrinkles as I come into contact with the hair on his legs. How did I ever think he was attractive? His sharp nose and angular cheekbones should have been enough to make me reconsider my stance, but I listened to the other girls obsessing over him and when he turned his attention on me…

Elijah starts. *It's far too easy to make him do that.*

I use the opportunity to kick his hip.

He stumbles, dropping the knife, and then runs.

With his knife in my hand, I follow Ephraim's training. The knife sails through the air, digging itself into Elijah's upper leg as he turns to look back at me. He curses, running with painful, hobbled steps. Blood drips down his leg as he moves toward the woods.

Looking back, I see Ephraim holding out his arm

across Hoyt's chest to stop him. "Let her go." My friend nods to me.

I turn, prepared to hunt down Elijah. I don't need to run—he's not going to get that far ahead—but I keep a quick pace as I track drops of blood on the ground the same way I look for signals from Grandmother.

The others follow several paces behind me, ready to back me up when I approach my prey. Orville calls out from atop Brisheet, telling us he plans to circle around in case we need him on the other end, though I doubt he'll be able to make it through the trees on the wide animal. The last thing I hear before I leave the area is that he's taking Blanch with him. Considering her injury, I think that's a wise choice.

Stepping into the woods is familiar. It's safe, even though it's in a town that I don't trust. With my friends trailing behind me and the town actively moving away from the fight that erupted at the show, I'm free to move without worrying about who else might be tracking me. Instead, I track down Elijah.

Leaves brush against my legs, my lace tights barely protecting me. I watch closely for anything that might cut into my flesh. The wind guides me, pushing at my back. I'm grateful for the breeze—it had been incredibly hot inside the tent and it whips the sweat off my back under my costume.

It doesn't take long to find my cape in a heap in the

middle of the pathway. I pick it up, wrapping it around my shoulders. I can't afford to carry it, and neither can the others. It flows out behind me in the breeze I'm creating as I jog through the woods barefoot.

Unlike the circus tent, the woods are filled with quieter sounds. Everything seems more natural out here. The breeze. The birds. The crunch of leaves beneath our feet. I barely notice the twigs piercing my feet as I move across the layers of decaying leaves on the forest floor.

The sound of heavy breathing catches my attention and I turn. Elijah tries to muffle his puffing but is unsuccessful—he made it quite a bit farther than I expected. One shoe sticks out from behind a tree where he's resting, attempting to cover himself with branches from the nearby bush.

"And here I thought you could pull off a disappearing act." I let my words sound like a song as the others surround the tree in a wide circle, leaving me to talk to Elijah alone. "I guess you're not as great of a magician as you thought. You talked a big game for such a sad little sideshow."

He glares at me, grimacing. One hand rests over his leg where he's trying to stop the bleeding. Red peeks out from around his fingers, dripping down the back of his knuckles until it falls to the dead leaves below.

Grandmother was right—*blood is silent.*

"I knew you weren't worth the trouble."

"Then why *did* you go to all this trouble, Elijah?" I ask, hand on my hip. "You could have worked with us and made a *real* name for yourself. Instead, you worked with Luther. How did you honestly think that would pay off?"

"Luther doesn't have staying power, Sienna. A few years from now, this would have all been mine."

"A creepy circus with reluctant captives as performers? How do you think that would have ended up?" I shift my shoulders, letting the cloak fall around my arms—he doesn't realize how many times the cloak hindered his plans, but I do.

"They all had reasons for cooperating," he insists. "And they like me better than Luther. *I* wasn't threatening their families. They were grateful to me and would have been grateful when I gave them jobs after I took over for Luther."

Delusional. That's the only explanation.

Elijah howls and cringes forward.

"You know, Ida could fix that for you. In addition to everything else she does, she's quite good with healing people's injuries—she's learned so much in her years with Samuel and his crew." I can feel my eyes spark as if I touched the end of an electric lamp before it was all the way removed from its power source. "You can come back with us, Elijah. At least you won't bleed out in the woods alone."

"You wouldn't be kind enough to let me die in peace," he growls. His eyes narrow.

"You're right; I wouldn't let you die alone. I'd sit here talking to you the entire time, drawing it out as long as possible. The good news is that you aren't going to die from that wound…unless I want you to. Now stop being ridiculous and get up—we have places to be."

"I'm not going back with you." He pushes himself up until he's balanced on one leg, holding himself up on the tree.

"I don't think you're getting back on your own." I raise an eyebrow at him. "You can let us help you back, or we can force you back, but either way, by this evening, you're the only one who is going to be in a cage."

"*You* looked better there," he snarls.

"I look better in *color*, you pathetic—"

"All right!" Ephraim interrupts, stomping over. "I've had enough. She hunted you down and you're going back into a cage where you will stay for a very long time, Elijah."

"I—"

"No. You keep your mouth shut, or we're handing you over to the local authorities." Ephraim twirls his knife in his hand for show. "I sincerely doubt you want to be locked up *here* in the town where you caused so much chaos. They're not going to be happy about the fight, or the animals running wild, or the fire that I'm sure they saw smoke from. When we tell them it's all your fault and it's because you've been abducting people to use in your show, I can only imagine how they'll react. Based on what I saw of the way they treated your performers when you let them walk around those cages, I have a feeling they'll have some creative forms of justice."

"Move," Hoyt demands.

Moving in behind Elijah, he wrenches the boy's arms back, tying them. Harriett stalks behind him, flashing a match to remind Elijah that she doesn't mind burning things down for the fun of it. The others walk behind them.

Josephine glances back at me, her features soft and delicate, clearly concerned about me. I'm surprised she stayed behind after she got Grandmother out of her cage.

"You okay?" Ephraim asks quietly.

"I'm fine," I whisper, feeling the day crash over me.

"Can I help you?" he whispers again. Turning both hands over, he offers to carry me back through the woods to spare my feet. I nod heavily, tiredness dragging over me.

Ephraim scoops me up in his arms, my hip pushing against his abdomen and chest, melting into the sculpted curves of his muscles. I rest my head against his shoulder, arm curved around his neck as I try to support part of my weight.

"Are your feet okay?" he asks.

"I'll be fine," I murmur into his collarbone. His breath hitches, jerking my forehead slightly where it rests against his neck. I lift my head up, suddenly amused as I remember our show on the silks. "You were pretty magnificent back there."

His lips quirk up as he catches my eye. "Yeah, well, tracking down the bad guys is kind of my specialty, Sienna."

"Oh, no, I meant up in the air." I really *am* impressed with what he pulled off. "How did you figure out how to do that?"

"You and I practiced enough. And I've tossed people around for the show before." He shrugs, jostling me. "Sorry."

"We hardly practiced enough for you to pull that off. Have you been working on that without me?"

"Let's just say I've been watching you closely enough to have a pretty good idea of what we could do together."

"Oh?" I raise an eyebrow. "What exactly can we do together?"

He grins.

"Was one of those things you thought we'd be good at the ending of our little show?" I tease, referring to the kiss.

"Oh, I *definitely* knew we'd be good at that." He blows a kiss at me and I have to fight a giggle.

We both dip as he ducks under a tree branch. I turn as

something catches Ephraim's eye ahead—Harriet. She gives us a look before turning around, and this time, *I* laugh.

"How bad do you think this is going to get?" I ask, nodding to our friends.

"Pretty bad, I'm going to guess. Orville has been rooting for us, but we'll never hear the end of it from Fannie and Hoyt."

"Good point."

"I'm pretty sure Ida will have some thoughts on this too."

"Ha!" I snort. "I'm sure she will."

"Is there anything I can do to sway her to my side on this?" Ephraim inquires. "I definitely didn't ask her permission before kissing her granddaughter, and that woman basically controls my future. I have a feeling I need to make it up to her before she spends the next five months making my life miserable to prove a point."

"You already rescued me, what more could she ask for?"

Ephraim laughs.

"What?" I ask, grinning.

"You rescued yourself, Red. *You*, Sienna, are one *star* act."

"I couldn't have done it without you, *Invincible Man*. Speaking of colors though, maybe we should dress you in red more often, what do you think?"

"If I have to perform in red, then *you*, have to spend a little time in blue during the show, my friend."

"*Friend?*" I challenge. His lips pull up in a wide smile. "What exactly does my appearance in blue require?"

"I can throw knives at you."

"No," I quickly cut him off.

"No?" he asks curiously.

"No. You have Fannie and Blanch for that."

"Fine, you can throw them at me and I'll catch them. It's the perfect crossover for my *Invincibility* act and knife throwing."

I consider it for a moment.

"That would probably require a lot of practice," I muse as we exit the forest. Orville has both elephants back under his watch. Our friends are turned, waiting for us to join them. Samuel calls out that we need to get back and check on Grandmother. Ephraim sets me down as Josephine runs for a pair of shoes for me.

"I wouldn't mind putting in a few extra hours every day until we get the routines down." He smiles at his cousin as Orville bumps into his arm. Orville looks around his cousin, giving me a look, trying to hold back a grin.

"Kiss her, or I will, Eph," Hoyt mumbles as he brushes by us, prepared to look for the animals the captives set free earlier so nothing happens with the townspeople.

Samuel splits us up, directing us on where to go to clean up Luther's mess. Everyone scurries off to help.

"Take her home, Ephraim. Make sure Ida is all right and then stand guard in case any of Luther's men decide to take matters into their own hands."

"What about the others?" I ask.

"They can join us if they like, or they're welcome to travel with us as far as they want until they reach home. I've let them all know they're welcome to stay with us this evening—we'll feed them and give them a place to rest until they can decide what they want to do." Samuel really does have a heart deep down somewhere. "They've all agreed to join us for this evening at least. Even a few of Luther's henchmen have requested jobs with us. They'll need to be tested first, of course."

"And the town?" Ephraim questions.

"If we get out of here quickly, they'll have no idea we were involved, and they won't find much of Luther's circus left. I've got Clarence and a few of the men dropping him off with the local authorities now though, with a full description of his transgressions.

"They're an odd bunch. I'm sure Luther will appreciate their unconventional methods. Elijah will be going with them."

Josephine reappears with shoes for me as Ephraim explains how I hunted Elijah down in the woods. I slip them on, grateful I no longer have to travel barefoot—I need my feet in one piece for tomorrow's final show before we move on from this place.

Elijah glares at us, hands bound in front of him, a cloth tied around his leg. His nostrils flare when I make eye contact with him.

Ephraim quietly takes my hand while he and Samuel talk, clearly ignoring Elijah so he doesn't beat him to a pulp.

"Good luck with Fannie," Josephine mutters as she backs away from me, keeping her voice low so only I hear her.

"Helpful, thank you."

"It's not *my* fault you felt compelled to kiss the most gorgeous man in this circus..." She rolls her eyes. "Aside from—"

She cuts her own words off as my eyebrows shoot up. I clutch the red cloak around my shoulders as I laugh, assuring her I'll find out whose name she almost said later this week.

"Come on," Ephraim tugs on my hand. "You can come with us, Josephine."

"Anyone want a ride?" Orville offers. Blanch holds his waist with her good arm as they sit on top of Brisheet. Caleo bends down to allow us on.

"I'm fine," Josephine runs off, leaving us standing there.

"She's on a mission," Ephraim muses.

"Let her go," Blanch calls, smiling. *She knows something.*

Ephraim helps me onto Caleo, and he and his cousin direct the elephants back toward our colorful circus tent. The lights will be sparkling by now as the sky starts to dim. My silks will be waiting for me, as will Grandmother, but I won't be performing this evening. The circus will be closed down to cater to the needs of the people we rescued today.

"Nice work today, Red." Ephraim leans back into my arms as I hold his waist. "You really drew some blood out there."

He references my grandmother's remarks about my silks. She'll be delighted when I tell her about what happened today. Perhaps blood *isn't* so silent all of the time.

"Nice work today, Invincible," I murmur into his ear. He purrs, turning his face to me slightly, no longer shy about his affections. "Want to practice on the silks tonight, *friend?*"

Maybe I can find out what that hair tug meant last night at the show. We clearly need to get better at working on our signals.

"I really don't think we have a choice if we want to get this right," he replies innocently as if I didn't have ulterior motives. "We need to start immediately...*without* an audience this time."

I fully agree.

ACKNOWLEDGMENTS

I had so much fun writing Sienna's story. Truth be told, when my advanced readers were real-time messaging me with their love for Elijah, I was delighted to watch them go from love to hate…for both me and him!

I'm definitely hoping to explore more of Sienna and Ephraim's world again soon. If it's something you'd like to see more of, please let me know…it might help me bump it up on my To Do list!

Special thanks to Jess and Elle for helping with this book baby.

Apologies to Yentl for tricking you with Elijah. Or, maybe I'm not sorry…definitely not sorry.

Extra special thanks to Morgana Alba, the Circus Siren, who consulted on this book to make sure I had all the technical stuff correct. You're the ultimate aerialist and mermaid siren, wrapped in a stunning girl boss package! I truly appreciate your help on this one!

And thank you to you, oh fabulous reader, for coming on this journey with me! I hope you enjoyed Red Riding Hood's twist as much as I did!

Be sure to check out my social media for an interactive, choose-your-own-adventure games, behind the scenes, and more for this story and my other stories!

Keep reading for a look at some of my other books I think you might really like too…some even have secrets!

Stay inspired,

-K.M. Robinson

ABOUT THE AUTHOR

K.M. Robinson is a storyteller who creates new worlds both in her writing and in her fine arts conceptual photography. She is a marketing, branding and social media strategy educator who is recognized at first sight by her very long hair. She is a creative who focuses on photography, videography, couture dress making, and writing to express the stories she needs to tell. She almost always has a camera within reach.

Visit her at her website: www.kmrobinsonbooks.com

CONNECT ON SOCIAL MEDIA

facebook.com/kmrobinsonbooks

instagram.com/kmrobinsonbooks

twitter.com/kmrobinsonbooks

Get free excerpts and full novels from K.M. Robinson at excerpt.kmrobinsonbooks.com

ALSO BY K.M. ROBINSON

The Golden Trilogy

Book One: Golden

Forged: A Golden Novella

Book Two: Locked

Book Three: Edge

The Complete Series Boxset/Omnibus with Tempered: an exclusive bonus novella

The Jaded Duology

Book One: Jaded

Book Two: Risen

The Complete Series Boxset/Omnibus with exclusive epilogue

The Siren Wars Saga

Book One: The Siren Wars

Book Two: Darker Depths

Book Three: Beyond The Shores

Origins of the Siren Wars: Prequel Novella

Book Four: Forbidden Waters (coming soon)

The Legends Chronicles

Along Came A Spider: A Prequel Novelette

And They'll Come Home: A Prequel Novelette

The Archives of Jack Frost Series

The Revolution of Jack Frost

The Redemption of Jack Frost (coming soon)

Stealing Steam Series

Book One: Lions and Lamps

Book Two: Pistons and Prisoners

Book Three: Railcars and Rulers

Top Hats and Telegraphs: A Prequel Novella

The Complete Series Boxset/Omnibus with Vambraces and Victories: an exclusive bonus novella

Virtually Sleeping Beauty: A Novella Retelling

The Goose Girl and The Artificial: A Novella Retelling

The Sinking: A Little Mermaid Novella Retelling

Cindrill: A Cinderella Assassin Novella Retelling

Sugarcoated: A Hansel and Gretel's Witch Novella Retelling

Blood Is Silent: A Red Riding Hood Circus Retelling

JADED: BOOK ONE OF THE JADED DUOLOGY

If the only way to stay alive was to convince your new husband not to murder you and make it look like an accident, could you do it?

At eighteen, Jade shouldn't have to be forced to marry the son of her father's enemy as part of a revenge plot for a failed rebellion. When she's thrown into the life of being the wife of the Commander's son and heir, her only hope for survival is convincing Roan Diamond to actually fall in love with her so that he doesn't kill her on his father's wishes.

While a dutiful son, Roan shouldn't have to trick his new wife into believing his family accepts her, but as the only one in a position to make the country believe Jade is part of their family, he will do what he has to before his family murders his young bride and makes it look like an accident to get back at Jade's father.

With half the country trying to protect Jade and the other half oblivious to the atrocities committed at the Commander's hand, it's a race to see who will win at a deadly game of cat and mouse.

One chooses life. One chooses death. In the midst of chaos, only one will succeed.

Now available!
Learn more about The Jaded Duology at
jadedinfo.kmrobinsonbooks.com

GOLDEN: BOOK ONE OF THE GOLDEN TRILOGY

Goldilocks wasn't naive. She was sent on a mission and Dov Baer is her new target.

When Auluria tricks the Baers into letting her into their home, they have no idea she's actually been sent by the enemy to destroy them. Intent on gathering information for her cousin to hand over to the Society seeking to destroy all of the rebel factions—including her own—she's willing to sacrifice Dov Baer to save her people... until she realizes her cousin lied to her.

Now that she's seen who Dov truly is, she has to decide between staying loyal to her only remaining family or protecting the man she's falling for. If her allegiances are discovered, either side could destroy her—assuming the Society doesn't get her first.

Available now!
Learn more about The Golden Trilogy at goldeninfo.
kmrobinsonbooks.com

**THE SIREN WARS: BOOK ONE OF THE
SIREN WARS SAGA**

War has hovered around the kingdom of Scylla for generations ever since the original sirens left the mer collection generations ago after nearly drowning the human prince. Over the years, select mermaids from the royal bloodline have been trained as spies to work for the reigning kings and queens, keeping the collection safe from sirens and humans.

Celena and her partner, Merrick, work covertly for the royals—not even her twin brother knows. When they discover the sirens have broken through the barriers the mer set up to keep the sirens out, Celena and her friends must race to the old kingdom of Metten to stop them from starting a war within their borders.

When she's dragged to the surface, Celena realizes that the war above the waters is as deadly as the one below the waves—and sacrificing herself may be the only way to protect her family.

The Siren Wars have only just begun.

Available now!
Learn more about The Siren Wars Saga at sirenwarsinfo.
kmrobinsonbooks.com

LIONS AND LAMPS: BOOK ONE OF THE STEALING STEAM SERIES

All wishes require sacrifice...*are you willing to pay the price?*

Cyra spent the last seven years being trained to steal an airship in a brutal competition that leaves the victor with millions. Last year, she won.

Aladdin spent the past year fighting to get enough money to take his mother away from Horallen after his father was murdered. Now, his evil uncle Kacper wants to force him into the competition and straight to his death inside the Collection Cave.

When Aladdin discovers a genie said to have been banished a century ago, the competition becomes even deadlier, and he knows he can't trust the girl who snuck into the competition this year...but Cyra might not survive his ruthlessness either in a game where only the lion's heart can win.

All wishes require sacrifice, and someone is going to pay the price for the Stourbridge.

Available now!
Learn more about The Stealing Steam Series at
lionsandlampsinfo.kmrobinsonbooks.com

ALONG CAME A SPIDER: THE FIRST PREQUEL NOVELETTE TO THE LEGENDS CHRONICLES

Little Hacker Muffet
sat on her tuffet
destroying her cords and Way.
Along came a hacker named Spider,
who sat down beside her
and frightened his opponent away.

WHEN FET, ONE OF THE MOST SKILLED HACKERS IN THE Legends, discovers her best friend and leader of her group has been abducted and held for ransom, she must escape unnoticed and find Peep before it's too late.

When Spider, a new recruit training to join her hacker ring, slips out with her and claims to have a plan to save her friend, Fet is forced to bring him along. As she discovers he's not who he claims to be, she faces grave danger and learns just how deadly a spider bite can be.

Now available!
Learn more about The Legends Chronicles at
acasinfo.kmrobinsonbooks.com

VIRTUALLY SLEEPING BEAUTY

To wake her up, he has to enter the game and help her beat it...

Surely the class president wouldn't illegally over-juice to stay in the virtual reality game citizens are allowed to play for four hours a day, but when Royce's aunt calls in a panic because her goddaughter hasn't left the game yet, his only option is to go inside the game and drag the girl out.

The golden knight quickly discovers the princess' absence in the real world isn't of her own doing—*she's trapped inside the game by unknown forces*—and if she can't escape soon, she could die for real outside of the game. He's even more shocked to discover that Rora outranks him inside of the game, which means she'll have to fight to *protect herself* from the evils locking her inside a dangerous world.

Can Rora and Royce work together to outsmart a vicious queen and evil magician, and defeat digital dragons, or will Rora slowly fade away until there's nothing left but an empty shell and the game ranking she will leave behind?

Now available!

Learn more about Virtually Sleeping Beauty at
vsbinfo.kmrobinsonbooks.com

THE REVOLUTION OF JACK FROST

No one inside the snow globe knows that Morozoko Industries is controlling their weather, testing them to form a stronger race that can survive the fall out from the bombs being dropped in the outside world—all they know is that they must survive the harsh Winter that lasts a month and use the few days of Spring, Summer, and Fall to gather enough supplies to survive.

When the seasons start shifting, Genesis and Jack know something is going on. As their team begins to find technology that they don't have access to inside their snow globe of a world, it begins to look more and more like one of their own is working against them.

· · ·

Genesis soon discovers Morozoko Industries, but when a foreign enemy tries to destroy their weather program to make sure their destructive life-altering bombs succeed in destroying the outside world, only one person can shut down the machine that is spinning out of control and save the lives of everyone inside the bunker—Jack.

Now available!
Learn more about The Revolution of Jack Frost at
jackfrostinfo.kmrobinsonbooks.com

THE GOOSE GIRL AND THE ARTIFICIAL

WHAT WOULD YOU DO IF YOUR ARTIFICIALLY INTELLIGENT handmaiden stole your identity?

Threatened by her Artificial, Arta, Princess Goselyn is forced to switch places and pretend she isn't human when she reaches Prince Corinth to negotiate a treaty they both need to be able to take their respective crowns one day. If she doesn't comply, her Artificial, controlled by her evil cousin, will not only kill Goselyn's mother, but Prince Corinth and his father as well.

Can the quiet princess outsmart a machine created to be more intelligent than she is, all while surviving the other

Artificials and robots working against her in the foreign palace, or will Corinth and his father find out and destroy her chance to save them all?

Learn more about The Goose Girl and The Artificial at goosegirlinfo.kmrobinsonbooks.com

THE SINKING

The sea witch wants to silence her, but not for the reason you think.

WHEN A QUIRKY OLDER WOMAN PAWNS A FANCY SEASHELL necklace at her mother's antique shop on the pier, Cara doesn't think much about the story the woman spins about the wearer turning into a mermaid.

On her way home, she accidentally drops the necklace into the ocean and is swept out to sea where she meets— a merman who volunteers to take her to his mother, the sea queen, to help her get her legs back.

. . .

Cara soon learns that it's Quay's eighteen birthday—a day that has been a curse for his family—and is meant to be one for her too. Now she must fight to survive the sea with Quay at her side.

Fans of The Little Mermaid will love this twisted take on the beloved story.

Now available!
Learn more about The Sinking at
thesinkinginfo.kmrobinsonbooks.com

CINDRILL

CINDERELLA IS AN ASSASSIN OUT TO MURDER THE PRINCE...
but he's hunting her too.

The nanobots Cindrill's master gives her to use as a mask allow her to slip into the ball wearing a face that isn't hers, but when the assassination attempt goes sideways, Prince Davin doesn't understand why her face changes when he injures her, slicing her foot open around a unique pair of shoes as she runs away.

When Cindrill runs into the prince the next day without her nanobot mask on, he doesn't recognize her, but immediately decides her skills will be useful on his hunt for the would-be-assassin woman who nearly killed his father and his fiancée the night before.

Both are tasked with the job of murdering the other, but things don't quite go as they had planned when Cindrill's master and Davian's fiancée interfere as the two try to decide whether or not to kill the other.

It's hard to recognize a woman when she uses technology to change her appearance, but Cindrill is going to use that to her full advantage as she destroys the prince. ***Will either survive?***

Now available!

Learn more about Cindrill at
cindrillinfo.kmrobinsonbooks.com

SUGARCOATED

Hansel and Gretel's witch was actually on their side...

ANNIKA'S JOB IS TO CREATE A CAKE TO MATCH THE CANDY-colored rooftops, nightly firework shows, and daily parades ending in unexpected executions for the mad king's ball, but her true mission is to sneak a thirteen-year-old assassin into the palace using her gift of illusions.

Hansel's job is to protect his little sister, Gretel, once she assassinates King Levin and ends the destruction in Candestrachen, using his power over light to rescue the young girl from the chaos her influence over life and death will create.

. . .

When the entire forest reconstructs itself under Gretel's command while trying to save herself from a king's guard, Hansel and Annika must put their feelings aside and ensure their plan holds true—even if it means one of them has to sacrifice themselves to protect the mission.

Her illusions were meant to save her....but not everyone will survive the assassination attempt.

Learn more about Sugarcoated at
sugarcoatedinfo.kmrobinsonbooks.com

www.ingramcontent.com/pod-product-compliance
Lightning Source LLC
Chambersburg PA
CBHW050409190726

48284CB00007BB/2491